THE TRAIL TO

A Historical Western Romance Novella

Crooked Creek

MK McCLINTOCK

TRAPPERS PEAK PUBLISHING

Published by Trappers Peak Publishing in the United States of America

www.mkmcclintock.com

Publisher's Note: This is a work of fiction. Names, characters, places, and incidents are fictitious. Locales and public names are sometimes used for atmospheric purposes. Any resemblance to actual people, living or dead, or to businesses, companies, events, institutions, or locales is completely coincidental.

The Trail to Crooked Creek; novella/MK McClintock

The Trail to Crooked Creek
A Crooked Creek Novella
by MK McClintock

The Trail to Crooked Creek is a tale of resilience, compassion, and the triumph of the human spirit set in the breathtaking and sometimes unforgiving landscape of post-Civil War Montana Territory.

Also in the Crooked Creek series
The Women of Crooked Creek
Christmas in Crooked Creek

Discover more at www.mkmcclintock.com

THE TRAIL TO CROOKED CREEK

Spring 1868
Twenty-five miles southwest of
Crooked Creek, Montana Territory

"IF YOU ARE GOING to kill us, I ask only that you do so swiftly, for the child's sake."

"What makes you think I have any intention of killing you?"

Leah Tennyson held her young charge close to her body beneath the security of her arms. Though strong, she did not harbor confidence in her ability to prevent the man from doing whatever he wished. If it took her last breath and her own life to secure Nelle's freedom, so be it.

He appeared from the shadows, his gait strong and gradual. She estimated his height at half a foot or taller than her five feet, five inches. Sitting on the ground as Leah and Nelle were and huddled against the narrow, white tree trunk, the man appeared more of a giant. A broadbrimmed felt hat shadowed his face, and in the fading light, Leah glimpsed only flashes of white teeth when he spoke.

"I don't intend to harm either of you." He held his hands high and to his sides to show the truth of his words. "I saw your fire but no horses."

Nelle kept her face tucked into Leah's shoulder. Leah whispered to the girl before rising slowly to her feet, using the tree for support. One step forward put her between the man and Nelle. "I am not a fool, sir, and do not mistake for me one."

"Duly noted, ma'am." He raised one hand to his head, and keeping the other arm out wide, removed the hat. Unruly hair, in a shade darker than Nelle's, though not quite brown, fell over his forehead before he brushed it back with a rough swipe of his hand. "The name's Wesley Davenport, ma'am."

She caught a hint of the South in his voice, though not as distinctly southern as the couple who brought a train car of orphans—and Leah—as far as Missouri. "Should your name mean anything to me, Mr. Davenport?"

"Not unless you're from Washington, Virginia, or thereabouts."

"You mean the capital of Washington?"

He smiled, and it came easily. "It's a common misunderstanding, ma'am, but no, Washington, Virginia. And I detect hints of Boston and maybe even a little British in your voice."

Nelle had stopped her fractured breathing from behind Leah's legs. She dared not glance down at the girl. Wesley did.

"You should be on your way, Mr. Davenport."

"Pardon my presumption, ma'am, but the pair of you don't look fit enough to make it to the next town."

"We've survived this long."

"May I?" Wesley pointed to the fire.

Leah gave him a quick nod. With early evening now upon them, she wanted to see more of his face. The light broke up the shadows when he crouched next to the meager fire and fed the flames with two more nearby sticks. She steeled her voice. "Where is the next town?"

"Crooked Creek. That's where I'm heading."

The stranger was not mistaken that they were unlikely to make it to the next town, not without help. Earlier in the day, Nelle had consumed the last of the insufficient provisions Leah had sneaked from the wagon before they escaped in the early hours five days ago.

"If you permit me, ma'am, I have jerky and a few biscuits left from this morning in my saddlebags. They're yours, if you'll accept them."

On cue, Nelle's stomach rumbled. Leah willed hers to silence. "Leah Tennyson. As opposed to ma'am."

"As in the poet?"

"Regrettably, no relation to Lord Tennyson, but yes. Were I capable of provoking such emotion with mere words, I would not be here."

He gave her a half salute. "Miss Tennyson." Without waiting for an answer to his earlier question about the food, Wesley whistled, the treble bringing forth a beautiful gray horse with a long, sleek neck and a mane and tail that shimmered in the firelight. Wesley rose from his crouched position, whispered to the animal, and lifted the flap of a saddlebag. Careful of his movements, he returned to the fire and tossed two cloth-wrapped bundles to the other side. They made a gentle landing near Leah's feet.

"What about you?"

"I've had my fill today. You go on ahead."

Leah gave up her wariness of Wesley Davenport long enough to pick up the bundles and kneel next to Nelle. She passed the young girl a biscuit first, admonishing her to take small bites. Enough water remained in the canteen to satisfy the girl's thirst every few seconds. "Thank you, Mr. Davenport. We ran out of supplies last evening, and I haven't the skill to hunt or forage. I did not realize the nearest town would be so far away."

Wesley set his hat on the saddle, crouched again, and added

more sticks to the fire. "That tends to happen, Miss Tennyson, when one is running away or hiding."

THE FIRE'S LIGHT CAST a wide enough glow to catch Leah's stiffening back and shoulders. Her mouth tightened into a straight line before one side sloped gently into what Wesley always thought of as a curious frown. "Don't worry. Whoever you're running from has nothing to do with me. I meant what I told you earlier: Crooked Creek is my destination."

"Virginia is a long way from here, Mr. Davenport."

Even with only the soft glow to see her by, Wesley studied her, from the soft brown hair coiled in a loose braid on her head to the hem of the purple-toned calico dress trimmed with lace. Only tips of black leather on her scuffed boots peeked from beneath the fabric. She wore a shawl but no coat. An oversized canvas coat covered most of the girl, and no bonnet hid the pale, blond braids.

Neither of them had any business being out here alone.

"So is Boston, Miss Tennyson." He waited for Leah to eat something, but she merely passed small portions to the girl. His next words came out soft, and the implication meant only for her. "You won't be any good to her if you're half starved. I'll hunt at first light."

She stiffened again. "I have not invited you to sleep at our fire, Mr. Davenport."

"I would not presume such an invitation." He pointed over his shoulder. "I'll stay over there a ways. Close enough to hear should you call out, far enough away so you can rest easy knowing I'm not at your side." Wesley drew back the edge of his black duster, withdrew one of his two Colts from a holster, and holding the grip with two fingers, leaned forward as far as he could to gently drop it at Leah's feet.

"All you do is point and shoot."

Leah stared at the pistol. The girl's eyes widened as she continued eating a rasher of jerky.

"It doesn't have teeth."

"You are wrong about that, sir."

Wesley considered she might be right, though not about him. "Either way, you'll feel better knowing you have it."

"You will not leave, even if I ask you?"

"Close enough to hear you, far enough so you can rest easy." Wesley stood, stomped the stiffness from his legs, and put his hat where it belonged. He untied his bedroll, set it on the ground, and said nothing more before he returned to the shadows.

Wesley found a cozy spot in a copse of aspens with their emerging green buds to welcome in spring. Despite the stretch into a new season, nights remained frigid. Damp chills and freezing nights were sensations he'd long ago grown accustomed to; the war had served up both year after year.

Leah Tennyson of Boston bore the delicate bones of a wealthy society miss, and the faint hint of England in her voice told him she'd been in that foreign country long enough for it to make an indelible impression on her upbringing.

"How the hell did you end up here, Miss Tennyson?" He didn't expect an answer from the darkness, though he wished for one just the same.

Leah had been careful to guard the young girl who couldn't be more than ten or eleven, as though she expected that's where his interest might lie. Wesley's stomach churned, for he knew too well that men of such ilk walked the earth when they should be at least six feet under it.

Wesley unsaddled his horse, brushed the gray down with a cloth he kept for that purpose, and settled on the ground next to the trees. He never hobbled the animal and trusted Revere to stay close through the night.

Images of and questions about Miss Leah Tennyson kept his mind awake even as his eyes shuttered to fight off exhaustion from a long day's ride. He'd spent the past two nights sleeping outdoors, and now he was eager for a bed, bath, and hot meal. He hoped to find all three in Crooked Creek, where his old comrade, Michael Donaghue, had found a home with his new wife. The letter, with an enclosed bank draft for eight hundred dollars, had arrived unexpectedly. He knew Michael to be an honorable man who paid his debts, yet he could not imagine what debt Michael felt he owed him.

No matter how far removed from life in Virginia and the only home he'd ever known, Crooked Creek sounded like the perfect place to start over. What, he wondered, would it take to convince Leah Tennyson to trust him to get her there safely?

DAWN'S CHORUS OF BIRDS brought Leah awake by slow degrees. Young leaves on the canopy of branches above diffused the morning light, and a blue sky painted with the faded remnants of an orange - and red-hued sunrise promised a clear, beautiful day for traveling.

She had missed the day's first light.

The thought of her legs carrying her another ten feet, let alone twenty-five more miles, brought her fully awake. Her stomach growled, and a hand pressed to it gave way to a concaveness not there before her journey west. The single biscuit she'd eaten last night, courtesy of Mr. Davenport, had barely skimmed the edge of her hunger.

Mr. Davenport.

Leah righted herself, draped an arm over a sleeping Nelle, and studied their surroundings. Birdsong echoed and mingled with a faint breeze rustling leaves and branches. Smoke fire and cooking meat invaded her senses next, and her stomach ached in response. A twig broke nearby, but when it came, the voice drew her attention to the trees to her right.

"Just me, Miss Tennyson."

Leah wiped residual sleep from her eyes and watched Wesley

Davenport approach. He led his horse with one hand, held cooked meat on a stick with the other, and waited for Leah to permit him to close the distance between them. She nodded, and he advanced. Leah thought he measured each step, and his gaze never veered from hers.

"I didn't want to wake you, so I prepared breakfast at my fire. I'll get this one going in a minute for you." He held out the stick with what he called breakfast to her.

"What is it?"

"Rabbit. I have fresh biscuits as well. It's not fancy fare but should tide everyone over until midday."

"You presume a great deal, Mr. Davenport. I have not invited you to travel with us."

He let his horse roam nearby to graze while he worked on the fire. "Could be I don't want you and the girl to starve or die from exposure. There are bound to be lions hereabouts, and with bears still coming out of hibernation, you don't want to be one of the first potential food sources they encounter."

Nelle stirred at Leah's side. She drew Nelle close and lifted the coat collar to cover her neck. "Do not think me ungrateful, Mr. Davenport. I am aware of the debt owed to you."

"You owe me nothing."

A flame grew in the firepit under Wesley's care, and the warmth soon reached Leah. Her wool shawl had proven unable to keep the chill from seeping into her bones at night. The longer they traveled, the colder the evenings became. She took comfort in the heavy Colt resting on her lap as she watched Wesley's efficient movements around the camp. Within minutes, he took the rabbit back and laid it on two large stones next to the fire's heat, and on another flat rock, he unwrapped a cloth to reveal four biscuits.

"They aren't much but will fill your bellies."

Nelle stirred again. This time, she yawned, sniffed the air, and her eyes eased open. "Leah?"

"I'm here, Nelle. Come, let us walk the sleep off, and then

you can eat." Leah rose to her knees and then awkwardly to her feet. She reached down to help the girl stand.

"Don't go so far I can't hear you."

Leah hesitated, then gave Wesley a nod before ushering Nelle deeper into the trees. Only when she could no longer see Wesley did they stop and take care of their own needs. She led Nelle to the nearby stream where they washed their hands, and Leah splashed some cool water on her face.

"Do you think he's like the other one, Leah?"

"No." Leah was startled to believe she meant it. "We will remain vigilant, but I believe he will help us. We need to find a town, Nelle. Do you understand? And we can't get there alone."

The girl nodded. "Do you think there will be pancakes and bacon?"

"Hopefully both and more." She smiled and smoothed a hand over Nelle's braids. "Do you want me to fix your hair before we return?"

At Nelle's nod, Leah deftly undid the messy braids, combed her fingers through the fair hair, and reworked the soft locks into a single braid. When they returned to the camp, Wesley was nowhere around, and he'd extinguished the fire.

"Where'd he go?"

Leah grasped Nelle's hand. "I don't know," she responded in a whisper.

WESLEY BACKTRACKED ONE-QUARTER mile and followed a deer trail to a rocky stream bed half that distance. He jumped across to disturb the rocks and leave a boot print in the damp soil on the narrow bank before backtracking again.

He planted his feet on a bed of pine needles and pebbles and waited. Four counts in and four out relaxed his breathing and muscles long enough for him to consider the worst-case scenario. Unfortunately, there were too many possibilities. A man, not a beast, followed his trail away from the small camp, but the misdirection wouldn't fool him for long.

When the stranger's footsteps faded down the first trail, Wesley returned to the camp, only to find it empty. "Miss Tennyson?" he whispered. Nothing. "Leah!" His whisper was harsher that time.

She emerged from behind a patch of blueberry shrubs showing clusters of new buds. The girl followed directly behind Leah. "I thought you'd left."

"I said I wouldn't." Wesley whistled for his horse, and it walked forward, water droplets dripping from its mouth. He grabbed the single canvas bag Leah had clutched in her arms and tied it to the saddle. "Revere can carry both of you for a while."

"Where were you?"

Wesley glanced pointedly at the girl. "I'll explain once we're away from here. Nelle, that's your name, right? Have you ever ridden a horse?"

The girl shook her head.

"Revere's gentle when he needs to be. Come on over here next to him." He held out his hands. "Is it all right if I lift you up?"

Nelle looked to Leah, who nodded after a second's hesitation. Wesley lifted the girl high and swung her into the saddle. "Your turn, Miss Tennyson."

Leah showed no reluctance this time. Before Wesley could help her, she slipped her foot into the stirrup, grabbed the saddle, and pulled herself up to sit behind Nelle.

"You've done that before."

She didn't answer him. "What about you?"

"I'll walk ahead a few feet, and Revere will follow. Keep quiet. I mean it, not a sound." Wesley passed her the cloth-wrapped biscuits next. Tucked in next to the soft bread were strips of meat from the rabbit. "Eat what you can while you ride."

Again, Leah nodded and Nelle mimicked her. Content with their agreement, though not entirely confident in their ability to remain silent for long, Wesley led the horse south toward Crooked Creek, opposite where he led the man following him.

They walked for nearly an hour before he looked back. Nelle slept against Leah's chest, and Leah's eyes scanned their surroundings, her gaze moving left to right and back again. He let the horse come abreast of him so he could speak with Leah.

"Who's looking for you?"

"Why do you think—"

"Someone came near the camp. I made enough noise to lead them away, but they'll have figured out by now the trail is cold and look for fresh tracks."

"I cannot speak of it, not right now." She glanced at Nelle.

"Fair enough. How dangerous is he?"

"He can hunt."

"That tells me he can use a gun. I want to know how much he wants to find you."

Leah's voice trembled when she whispered, "He does not want to find me."

Wesley's gaze flitted to Nelle. "I see." And he did. The war left deep scars on his mind and soul, and not all of them were of men killing men. That was hard enough to reconcile. Images seared into his thoughts were those of the women protecting their young sons and daughters and young men and boys with bullets in their chests because they couldn't stop soldiers, bandits, and ruffians from taking what they wanted.

"Mr. Davenport?"

"It's Wesley."

Leah did not quibble over the lack of formality. "Thank you."

"What brought you west, Miss Tennyson?"

She accepted his abrupt change in subject, for which he was grateful.

"You may call me Leah. It seems right somehow." She

readjusted her seat and moved Nelle's head off her arm. It often took weeks or months before she permitted a man to use her given name, but under the circumstances, she needed to believe they were more than strangers. "I went to work at a Quaker school for orphans outside of Boston when I was eighteen. My aunt and uncle raised me for two years before then, after which he agreed to finance my education. I returned to the school as a teacher and was there until the couple who ran it brought the children west."

Wesley suspected he was getting a severely pared-down version of her story. "Another orphan train. Too damn many of them." He glanced up at her. "Sorry."

"You do not need to apologize. I would have disagreed with you before, but now . . ."

They each looked at Nelle again, and he let the subject drop because the girl stirred awake.

"Are we there?"

Leah and Wesley smiled. "Not yet," Leah said.

"We'll stop in another hour to rest." Wesley walked ahead again, leaving Leah and Nelle to quiet conversation. They stopped for a respite on the edge of a meadow surrounded by mountains on one side and trees on the other. Jerky and water tied them over, but Wesley knew they would need more substantial fare if they were going to make it. From the faint dark smudges under their eyes and the hollowness of their cheeks, he suspected they'd been rationing for days. Alone, he would have covered the last twenty-five miles of his trek to Crooked Creek in a single day. With Leah and Nelle, it would be sometime tomorrow before they reached the town.

Wesley knew where to go, thanks to a grizzled-face man at the last trading post where he stopped for supplies. Crooked Creek was not yet on readily available maps, and most folks didn't need one. White Eagle Ranch was well-enough known in the region, and the mine north of town employed several men, who sometimes moved on after a season or two. The trading post operator mentioned that a fancy eastern lady owned a hotel in town, and the café served up the best meatloaf in the territory.

Crooked Creek sounded as near to perfect as Wesley hoped to find. Whether Leah Tennyson agreed after she saw the place for herself remained a question. When they finally made camp for the night, Wesley built a small pit and started a fire. He left Revere with them while he hunted for their supper, and when he returned half an hour later with a grouse he'd already plucked, Leah had two piles of rocks stacked on top of each other with a long stick lying across the top. It was crude, but as long as the rocks didn't tumble, Wesley thought it might work.

"I don't know how to set it up the other way."

He smiled. "This works. Thank you." Wesley prepared and cooked the bird while Leah and Nelle saw to their personal needs away from the small camp. When they returned, Leah laid the bedroll next to a tree trunk. He almost told them to move it closer to the fire, then realized Leah probably planned to sleep against the tree.

"I'll keep watch tonight. You'll be warmer and sleep better closer to the heat."

Leah didn't argue, though Wesley expected she might once Nelle fell asleep. That opportunity came sooner than he expected. Once they'd eaten their fill—Leah not nearly enough —Nelle curled up on the bedroll and slept. Leah surprised him moments later by joining him on the log he had rolled near the fire.

"You are a patient man, Mr.—Wesley."

"Not always."

"I shouldn't believe in you. I do, though I concede a wise woman would not put faith in a stranger."

"Under most circumstances, I'd agree. In fact, I'll caution you not to trust anyone else you meet out here, at least until we reach town."

"Only you, then?"

Wesley grinned. "The hint of sarcasm in your voice tells me you're a wise woman. You're aware that placing your confidence in me encompasses some risk. However, you also recognize that you and your charge are at considerably less risk with me than if you were alone."

Leah shook her head and gave him a sideways look. "I am impressed at your insight yet troubled that it is true. A wise person would also know that should you have meant us harm, I could not have stopped you."

"We'll have to disagree there. You reminded me of a mama bear protecting a cub, and that's not a skirmish I'd want to chance."

Leah watched the flames dance and flicker. "We got to the end of the line in Missouri when a notice went out about the adoptions. I suppose they figured that was far enough west for the children. A young couple, perhaps in their mid-twenties, adopted Nelle. The wife, Lara, was well along with their first child. Her husband, Hank, seemed nice enough at first."

Wesley poked a stick at a log in the fire. "We're a lot of miles and cold nights from Missouri. How did you end up traveling with them?"

"The wife couldn't do much in her condition, and when they said they were heading to Montana to mine for gold, I volunteered to join them in hopes of securing a teaching position upon our arrival."

Wesley suspected it was not the draw of a long and dangerous journey north that compelled her to volunteer. "You got as far as Montana Territory, so what happened?"

"He wanted to teach Nelle how to hunt and offered to take her with him while I looked after his wife. The way he looked at her—"

It did not take a vivid imagination to deduce what could have happened to Nelle alone in the wilderness with the man. Wesley's hand tightened around the stick.

"The law calls it kidnapping." Leah gripped fabric from her

skirt into a fist. "What I've done. A lawman will be obligated to arrest me and return Nelle."

"The law isn't always right." He snapped the end of the stick and tossed it on the flames. "We'll be in Crooked Creek tomorrow. They have a sheriff and, from what I heard, a part-time U.S. Marshal."

"They can't know the truth. The law—"

"You can't run forever, Leah. Not out here. If exposure or wild animals don't get you first—"

"Yes, I know." Leah bent at the waist and rested her face in her palms. Her shoulders weren't moving, and she made no sound, so he assumed she wasn't crying. Wesley's mother used to affect a similar pose when she was deep in thought and working out a potential problem before sharing a solution with anyone else.

"Get some sleep, Leah. You'll need it."

***

WARMTH ENVELOPED LEAH IN its cocoon, and she snuggled deeper into the comforting glow of whatever source her dream state could not discern. She rolled onto her back and flicked a hand at the tickle on her shoulder. When a hand covered her mouth and a voice close to her ear whispered, "Stay quiet, Leah," her eyes opened, and she flailed in her effort to sit up.

Wesley pointed to Nelle, who slumbered peacefully. Leah nodded, and Wesley removed his hand.

She leaned close enough to him so her voice wouldn't carry. "Someone is out there?"

"Yes. Will Nelle awaken if I move her?"

Leah studied the young girl's unguarded expression in the depths of sleep. "I'll cover her mouth if it comes to it. As you well know, it's effective."

Wesley gathered Nelle into his arms, and with Leah near the girl's head, he carried her to the horse. Leah climbed into the saddle first, sitting astride, and cradled a sleeping Nelle in her arms when Wesley laid her in Leah's lap. He disappeared from view for a few seconds and returned with the bedroll. Once he tied it to the saddle, Wesley led Revere away from the camp.

"How well do you ride?"

Leah stared at the back of his head, uncertain if she had heard correctly. He eased his steps until he walked abreast of where she sat in the saddle.

"Can you ride, Leah?"

"Yes."

Wesley helped maneuver Nelle until she sat with one leg on either side of the horse. The girl eased awake and clasped the saddle horn. "Revere will follow your lead. A gentle tug on the reins or a light press with either knee will tell him what to do." Wesley gave a light pat to Revere's hindquarters and drifted into the darkness behind them.

"Leah." Nelle's voice trembled.

"We need to stay quiet. Can you do that for me?"

"We're all alone."

Leah couldn't see beyond the next tree. She kept her voice in a whisper and leaned her head down. "No, we're not. We have Revere with us, who must be named for the great Paul Revere, a brave and resilient man who escaped far worse scrapes than we are in now. And Mr. Davenport would never leave such a magnificent horse behind, would he?"

The girl shook her head and leaned against Leah. "I'm so tired, Leah."

"I know, sweet one. So am I." Revere navigated through the trees and must have found a trail, for they traveled a space wide enough to keep their legs from rubbing against shrubs and tree trunks. She prayed the animal had a better sense of direction than she did—and added an extra prayer that he could find his way back to Wesley.

Soft hues of orange and yellow heralded sunrise and a new day. Still, there was no sign of Wesley. Leah's light tug on the reins brought Revere to a stop. White puffs emerged from the horse's nostrils when he breathed out, yet he stayed quiet and appeared to look around. Revere's ears stood erect, and every few seconds, one ear turned backward, listening, while the other remained forward. The animal tensed beneath them, though Leah did not hear or sense whatever he did.

She almost squeezed her knees to urge the horse onward at the sound of cracking twigs behind them. The familiar voice halted the instinctive response. "Leah."

"Wesley?"

She turned the horse enough to watch Wesley's approach on a reddish-brown bay. Once upon them, he dismounted, walked around the horse, and held his arms out to help Nelle down first. When Leah swung a leg over the horse, her leg still in the stirrup and depleted of strength, she could not hold the whole of her weight. Wesley's arms encircled her before she fell, and cradled against him, with her back to his chest, he lowered her to the ground. His hold lasted long enough to ensure she could stand on her own. "We'll rest here for fifteen minutes. I estimate we're about half a day's ride from Crooked Creek."

He offered no explanation for his long absence or the appearance of an extra horse. Nor did he seem at all affected by the closeness of their bodies seconds ago while she fought to release the sudden tightness in her chest. When she moved, her legs tingled as the blood rushed through them. "Nelle and I should walk for a while."

"Maybe later."

Leah met his gaze. He shuttered his emotions so she could not discern whatever he held inside. Her gaze lowered to the center of his shirt, not covered by the duster. A small red mark, unnoticeable had she not been studying him so closely, stained the fabric. A tremble coursed through her, and she stared until Nelle tugged on her sleeve.

"I have to go, Leah," she whispered.

Wesley turned his attention to the animals. "Stretch your

legs. We'll rest long enough for you both to eat, then we'll head out."

"Come along." Leah led her into the trees and waited on the other side of a shrub. Once they were back at the horses, Nelle settled onto a log and accepted a biscuit. She halfheartedly nibbled on the soft bread, hunger no longer a match for exhaustion.

Wesley latched his hand around Leah's arm and led her several feet away but kept them visible to Nelle and his voice low. "What did Hank look like?"

Her eyes narrowed. "Hank? Average, I suppose. An inch or two shorter than you, medium-brown hair, brown eyes. There was nothing at all remarkable about him. Why?"

Wesley's jaw tightened. "That's not who was following us."

Leah felt another tremble and wrapped her arms around her middle. "Was?"

"Listen, Leah—"

"No, I don't want to hear what happened." She darted a glance at Nelle, who appeared to be falling asleep, her body lilting a little. "The blood on your shirt."

"He gave me no choice."

Had she mistrusted this man? Even as the question flitted into Leah's thoughts, she dismissed it. No, she had not mislaid her trust, at least regarding her and Nelle's safety. "Do you know what he wanted?"

"You and Nelle are the only things worth stealing out here."

A lump formed in her throat, and she forced it down. "And Revere."

Wesley's mouth lifted slightly to the right. "I didn't think you'd appreciate that."

"I am aware of the worth of a fine steed like Revere. You named him after Paul Revere, did you not? That is what I told Nelle."

Wesley nodded. "He deserved a worthy name. Listen, Leah, I don't know why the man was following us, and he didn't say anything worthwhile before . . . we need to get to Crooked Creek as quickly as possible. The bay is a sound animal in good health and strong enough to carry you and Nelle."

Leah recalled the ship crossing from England that tore all happiness from her life and believed if the great Atlantic Ocean could not destroy her resolve, neither would whatever forces sought to harm them now.

GENTLE RAIN AND THE soft suction of fresh mud beneath the horses' hooves joined them as they rode the last half-mile toward Crooked Creek. Wesley's hat sat atop Leah's damp head, with wisps of cinnamon-brown hair curling against her neck. His duster covered her back and shoulders and offered additional protection for Nelle, who still wore the oversized canvas coat.

Wesley rode alongside them rather than in front to ensure Leah could control the horse in the changeable weather. She had proven a capable horsewoman, and with each passing mile, Wesley credited her with even more strength and determination than he had originally expected. Weary yet not beaten, she offered him a grim smile from beneath the felt hat beaded with moisture.

He moved his horse in front of Leah's without warning and withdrew his Colt revolver from its leather holster. Ponderosas reached toward the heavens on their right. On their left, a landscape of sodden grass, delicate purple shoots of wild lilies, and half a dozen boulders covered the distance between them and the thick forest of trees a quarter mile away. The openness, while at once beautiful, left them vulnerable.

Wesley doubted anyone could have caught up by now or overtaken them, given they were traveling the only road into Crooked Creek. There had been no sign of the man following them having a partner. Leah and Nelle remained quiet, for which he silently thanked them as he studied their surroundings.

He nodded his head toward the towering trees. Leah's horse brushed against his leg as she navigated the animal away. Wesley waited, watched, and listened the best he could through the droplets falling around him. He pressed his finger to the Colt's hammer and kept the digit a hairbreadth from the trigger, in readiness to fire. His special talent and speed with weapons—as his first captain called it—was both a blessing and curse. "Show yourself now!"

From between two great ponderosas twenty feet ahead of him emerged the head of a tall black horse, and seconds later, its rider, sitting straight in the saddle with his head up and eyes forward. Rain drops gathered and fell from the brim of his hat, and his duster repelled more of the water than it soaked in.

"I applaud your caution, but it's unnecessary, at least right now."

The man, who Wesley estimated to be two or three inches over his own six feet, pulled back the right edge of his duster to reveal a silver badge engraved with: SHERIFF. "Peyton Sawyer."

"Wesley Davenport." He lowered his gun. "Do you make a habit of hiding in the trees, Sheriff?"

Peyton's mouth twitched. "Only when I'm tracking an inconsiderate foe. In this case, a lion with an appetite for sheep." He pointed to the pistol in Wesley's hands. "You know how to use that?"

Wesley holstered the pistol. "When necessary."

"And the rifle in the fine leather scabbard?"

"Whitworth."

"The rifle of snipers. Good to know." Peyton eased his horse closer until the two animals stood five feet apart. "You alone?"

"You already know I'm not." Wesley glanced toward the trees. "It's safe, Leah."

Peyton shook his head. "You're too trusting. The badge could be fake."

Wesley surprised a smile from himself. "True. As it happens, your name is not unknown to me." Trust or not, he kept Revere between the sheriff and Leah when they appeared from an opening in the trees.

The earlier softness around Peyton's eyes tightened at the sight of woman and young girl huddled on the horse. "Is Crooked Creek your destination?"

Wesley nodded. "It is, and I expect we'll have company before too long."

Peyton nodded as though understanding. It appeared the man had a lot to say and even more questions, but one more quick perusal of Wesley's companions kept his tongue silent. "We'll settle them at the inn, then you and I will talk."

"That's fine, Sheriff. Lead the way."

Wesley and Leah rode abreast of each other while Peyton kept the lead. Leah brought her horse close enough to Wesley's for her leg to brush his and whispered, "How do you know you can believe him?"

"A friend mentioned the name, and the proprietor at the trading post I stopped did as well. If you're uncomfortable—"

"If you had never heard his name, would you still follow him?"

Surprised at the intelligence of her question, though realizing there's no reason he should be, Wesley nodded, and confirmed with, "I would."

"All right."

Their small party let all conversation lapse until rain gave way to an ethereal mist and the first signs of civilization appeared. The road widened and cut a path through the town of Crooked Creek, dividing two rows of structures of varying heights. The sun remained behind a heavy blanket of gray clouds, which cast what might have been an overwhelming gloominess to the town were it not for lamplight in windows and an unexpected bustle.

They passed folks who tipped their hats or looked on with curious abandon. The blacksmith's hammer against iron paused long enough for the brawny man with a friendly smile to wave and call out to Sheriff Sawyer.

Leah kept her horse as close to Wesley as was comfortable, and one arm remained wrapped around Nelle, who had fallen asleep a few minutes before they arrived in town.

She worried her lower lip between her teeth. Wesley chanced touching her and rested a hand on her covered arm. "You'll be safe here. You both will."

"He'll find us, Wesley. After we rest, I think it's best we move on."

Wesley wondered how he hadn't found them already.

"Up ahead," Peyton called out.

"We'll talk later." Wesley squeezed her arm, then dropped his hand. "Food and rest first." He indicated Nelle with a quick nod, and Leah closed her eyes briefly as if to agree out of sheer exhaustion.

Peyton dismounted in front of what Wesley considered a smaller version of some mansions typical in the eastern states. An impressive structure that rose three levels, the inn spanned the width of a quarter acre and boasted a wide, covered porch built to the full length of the house. Smoke from hearths rose from two chimneys, and when the front door opened, the mingled scents of spices, yeast, and meat wafted into the air.

Wesley kept to his saddle until a woman exited the door, leaving it ajar behind her, and smiled at Peyton.

"Did you find the lion?"

"Tracked it well away from here, but no telling it if it will return." Peyton walked up the wide porch steps, removed his hat, and placed a kiss on the woman's cheek. "Brought you a few guests."

"We have room."

Wesley dismounted, rounded his horse, and lifted Nelle from the saddle. He steadied the girl, then slipped his hands beneath the borrowed duster, settled them at Leah's waist, and lowered her to the ground. Her horsemanship aside, she was obviously not accustomed to spending all day in a saddle. She rested an arm gently on Nelle's shoulders and did not shrink away from the gentle pressure of Wesley's hand on her back.

Once they ascended the steps, Peyton made the introductions, at least as far as he could. "Clara Donoghue, this is Wesley Davenport—"

Peyton's brows raised at Clara's quick breath intake and immediate smile. "You know him?"

She shook her head. "No, but Michael does. You are Wesley Davenport of Virginia?"

Wesley returned her smile. "Yes, ma'am. I expect there will be many questions, and I'll answer them as best I can. The sheriff has plenty of his own he's been holding back. This is Miss Leah Tennyson and her charge, Nelle. I'd be obliged, Mrs. Donoghue, if you'd see to them. It's been a rough few days on the trail."

"Please, you are all welcome to call me Clara." She held out a hand to Leah, who readily accepted the warm gesture. "If you'll both come with me."

Leah paused at the doorway and said to Sheriff Sawyer, "Mr. Davenport will have many of your answers, Sheriff. However, I will require some of your time once Nelle is situated."

Peyton nodded, and when the women were safely on the other side of the door, he focused his attention on Wesley. "I expect you're hankering for a good meal and warm bed as much as they are, but I'll need a few answers. We can take care of it now or after you've eaten."

"You strike me as a reasonable man, Sheriff. Probably even friendly to most folks—until they cross you or someone you love. Why don't you ask me the first question, and we'll go from there?"

"Fair enough. How do you know Michael Donaghue?"

"We shared a few campfires and a lot of bland meals."

"Whitworth rifle," Peyton murmured. "Sharpshooter?"

Wesley nodded, then asked, "How well do you know him?"

"Well enough." Peyton's mouth rose at the edges into a slight smile. "He's my brother-in-law. Now answer this: Who are the woman and child to you, because I'd wager my favorite Colt that they aren't kin."

Wesley fisted his hand to draw the unexpected pressure away from his chest. "I'll take that meal and bath first."

CLARA'S WILLOWY FRAME HID a deceptively strong woman, and her grace and kindness obscured a determination so fierce, Leah had little choice but to acquiesce to the woman's attention.

In less time than Leah's exhausted mind could formulate explanations as to how they came to be in Crooked Creek's beautiful inn with a strange man escorting them, Clara had Nelle soaking in a warm bath and a change of clothes set out for them both.

"Briley can shorten the hem and sleeves on two other dresses, but this one should do for now." The cotton dress in a blue-and-gray stripe with pearl buttons up the front and full skirt looked better suited to afternoon tea in a city than quiet living in a mountain town. "Your generosity is humbling, Mrs. Donoghue, but I cannot accept this."

"Again, please call me Clara, and yes, you can." Clara smoothed the sleeves, then laid out a pristine cotton chemise and petticoat next to the dress. Both garments bore creases and smelled faintly of lavender. She next laid out a pretty red dress with lace trim in a smaller size and added new undergarments. "You will do me a favor by wearing them. My mother sends a small crate of dresses and accoutrements for my daughter and me every few months from Connecticut. After I married, she included clothes for my husband as well." Clara brushed a stray, honey-colored lock of hair from her forehead. "What clothes I can't give away sit in a bureau going to waste."

Another woman entered the room carrying a stack of towels and immediately crossed to the adjoining bathing room.

"That is Susan. I will introduce you when she comes back through. She makes the best apple pie and honey wheat bread ever."

Clara asked her no question, so Leah offered no response. Her fingers itched to touch the clean dress with its pretty stripes, but she refrained, knowing her hands still bore evidence of the hard week on the trail.

"How long have you been in America?"

Leah finally gave Clara her full attention. "How did you know?"

"My grandmother arrived from England when she was ten years old, and her voice always hinted at her previous life. You sound much like I remember she did."

"We left England soon after I turned sixteen."

"We?"

"I traveled with my parents." Leah's jaw tightened. She heard the terseness in her words and regretted them.

Clara's soft smile hinted at understanding. "You will discover, Leah, that most individuals who find their way to Crooked Creek have a history and story to tell . . . in their own time."

Leah turned her head to look over her shoulder at the bathing room. Nelle's light laughter helped soothe the ragged edges of her heart. A breath shuddered up from her lungs to be released with a heavy sigh. "I have to trust someone."

"Mr. Davenport?"

"Yes." Leah nodded and pushed back the tears rimming her eyelids. "He saved us, but . . ."

Clara gently held both of Leah's arms and rubbed warmth into her flesh beneath the soiled sleeves. "But what?"

"This is *his* destination, and I cannot impose on him further."

"To do what?" Clara dropped her hands and lowered her

voice. "To leave? You only arrived, and neither you nor Nelle are in any condition to travel for at least a week. And go where?" When Leah didn't answer, Clara added, "Whatever your circumstances, you would not be mired in them if you had another choice."

Knowing Clara spoke the truth, yet unwilling to give up, Leah nodded once and held back the dam of tears edging to escape. "You are right. We need to rest." She willed embarrassment not to creep into her voice when she said, "I am without the means to pay you for the lodging, meals, and clothes."

"That isn't—"

Leah shook her head. "It is. We cannot stay long, but I need to be of use while we are here. I'm a fair cook and can help in the kitchen, and I'm strong enough to clean and work in the garden."

Clara studied her for what must have been a full minute. During that time, she fiddled with the dresses while Leah waited and wondered if the desperation she'd heard in her voice was a product of her imagination.

The seconds passed, and Nelle emerged from the bathing room, freshly scrubbed and her hair combed. She wore a cotton nightgown with frills at the sleeves and neck. Nelle's hesitant smile washed away her unease, and she vowed to do whatever was necessary to help the young girl regain her full smile.

Susan followed with the used towels and beamed at Nelle. "Pretty as a picture. Now, crawl under those covers in that cozy bed, and I'll bring you a tray of food."

Nelle looked to Leah first, who merely nodded, and with eagerness clashing with hesitation, the young girl slid beneath the covers and breathed deeply.

Clara carefully picked up the dress and undergarments she'd selected for Leah, motioned with her head toward the bedroom door, and Susan followed her into the hall. Leah glanced their way, then to Nelle. "I won't be long."

"All right." Nelle pressed her head to the pillow. Before Leah reached the door, Nelle sat up and forward. "Leah?"

Leah turned, her grip on the door handle. "Yes, dear?"

"Can we stay here?"

Sorrow and yearning filled Leah's heart, and she knew not which one she'd have to choose. "Right now, there is nowhere else we need to be." It wasn't an answer, and the easing of Nelle's smile into a straight line told Leah the girl understood she could not make such a promise. Leah also knew Nelle's young and fragile mind did not understand why.

When Leah entered the hall, Clara, leaning against the wall, stepped forward. "A bath is drawn for you in the room next to Nelle's. I've already laid the clothes out, including a nightgown and robe. Please, they are a gift," she added in haste, when Leah opened her mouth to protest.

"Thank you."

Clara smiled. "You're welcome."

"You will not ask?"

"Clara stared at the door to Nelle's room for several seconds. "You aren't the first woman to run away from a moment in their past and end up here."

Leah clutched a fist over her chest. "It is not my past that I fear."

Clara rubbed a hand over Leah's arm. "Then whatever it is you do fear, for your sake and Nelle's, I pray you find another store of the courage that brought you this far. You are only alone in your troubles if you choose to be."

When Clara turned, Leah stopped her with a fleeting touch. "We are strangers, and no one here deserves the trouble that might come with us."

"Do you have family left?"

Leah drew her hand back to her side. "No one is eager to receive a telegram from me." She thought the words cruel even as she spoke them. Her aunt's kindness had helped Leah through the worst years of her life.

"That is not quite what I asked, but no matter." Clara patted Leah's arm, and her smile brightened her countenance. "If you want to sleep, I'll bring up a tray."

"Besides a desire to be rid of trail grime, I long to sleep for a month. However, I'll come downstairs first. I want to speak with the sheriff so he knows what to expect."

"You mean *who* to expect?" At Leah's nod, Clara exhaled a deep breath. "There are a few other women to whom I'd like to introduce you."

"To what end? I will not be here long."

"Meet them first, then you will understand."

WITHOUT DIRT AND SWEAT under his clothes and mud caked to his boots, Wesley declared himself presentable enough to sit at a table in Clara's dining room. He kept to the sitting room, hoping Leah might find her way downstairs. When another quarter hour passed, Clara sought him out.

"She may appreciate the gentlemanly act, but Leah won't thank you for going hungry while you await her. She'll be down soon enough."

Too many scents wafted from somewhere in the back of the inn for Wesley to discern one from the next. "Has she eaten?"

A few wisps of fair hair slipped from the twist at Clara's nape when she tilted her head slightly and studied him. "What is she to you, Mr. Davenport?"

"I mean her no harm, if that's what you're wondering, Mrs. Donoghue."

A smile softened Clara's next words. "If I suspected that, you'd be sitting in Sheriff Sawyer's jail. I expect Michael's return in two hours, and you will need your strength to withstand Peyton's questions. Leah insists on coming downstairs to eat, but Susan brought a tray up to Nelle and added some extra for Leah."

Wesley scratched the side of his face and wished he'd taken time to shave. "Thank you, Mrs. Donoghue."

"Clara, please. I insist."

Wesley withdrew a small leather pouch of coins and surprised Clara by taking up her hand and folding her fingers over it. "You and Michael will want to argue, but this is important to me. Michael will understand, though he won't accept this as graciously as you. I'd be obliged if you'd take this to cover lodging and board for myself, plus Leah and Nelle."

Clara stared at the pouch, then up at him. Her mouth opened and closed before she puffed out a breath. "Are you a lawyer?"

Wesley chuckled. "No, ma'am."

"Then you have missed your calling." Clara slipped the pouch into her skirt pocket. "I will leave you to my husband. Please, sit. Peyton will be along shortly."

No sooner had Clara left and Wesley relaxed into one of the slat-backed chairs that Sheriff Sawyer entered the dining room, sans hat and coat, and walked a direct route to Wesley's table. It was an in-between time of day, and no one else was present.

"You look more human, at least, and not as undernourished as your traveling companions." Peyton sat in the chair opposite Wesley. "How long have you been together?"

"You don't waste time."

"No, he does not." The proprietress herself carried a tray from the kitchen and laid out a plate piled high with a thick cut of beef, fried potatoes, stewed carrots, two slices of thick sourdough bread, and a side of applesauce with cinnamon. She added a glass of water and a mug of coffee to the offerings. In front of Peyton, Clara set a cup of dark coffee and a slice of apple pie. "There is plenty of pie if you have room after your meal, Mr. Davenport."

"Wesley."

She tilted her head briefly, smiled, and then darted a fierce look to the sheriff. "Be kind, Peyton." Clara walked lightly back to the kitchen, leaving Peyton and Wesley alone.

Wesley picked up his fork and nodded toward the swinging doors Clara passed through seconds ago. "She terrifies you."

Peyton's unexpected laugh filled the ample space. "They all do."

"They?"

"The women of our town, four of them especially—my wife included. You'll understand when you meet the others." Peyton sipped at the coffee, blew a little on the surface, and drank deeply. "You haven't answered my question."

"No, I haven't." Wesley speared three sliced potatoes first and savored the herbs and pepper the cook had used to season them before chewing. He sampled a little of everything before he stopped long enough to speak again. "You're more patient than I expected."

"Not usually."

"Then you're either humoring me because I'm intentionally putting you off, or you are kind enough to let me enjoy my meal."

Peyton's mouth twitched. "A little of both."

"Fair enough. And two days is the answer to your question. Specifically, two nights and nearly two days." Wesley took a long swallow from a glass of water. "I found them about twenty-five miles southwest of here. They'd already been on their own for several days. Miss Tennyson can enlighten you more about the time before I encountered them."

"She's running."

Wesley confirmed with a nod, though Peyton had not posed it as a question. "She's protecting Nelle."

Peyton straightened in the chair. "All right. From whom?"

"Hank is the only name I have."

"Where's she from?"

"Her story isn't mine to tell, Sheriff. If Miss Tennyson wants you to know, she'll tell you herself. I only care that they are safe.

This Hank Duggan had plenty of time to catch up, even before I found them. That he hasn't yet is surprising and a bit unsettling."

"Unless he doesn't care as much as Miss Tennyson believes."

A flash of Leah's fear filled Wesley's vision. Her taut features and the fierce protectiveness over Nelle when he first entered her tiny camp hovered on the edge of his sight. "No. Make no mistake, Sheriff, he cares."

Peyton finished his coffee, pushed his mug across the heavy linen tablecloth, and smoothed his hand over where it puckered. "They're safe here."

Wesley left Peyton to his further assessments and quiet thoughts while he finished his potatoes and half his meat and applesauce. He eyed the apple pie Peyton had yet to sample and thought perhaps after the evening meal, his stomach might better appreciate a slice. "I heard there's a mine nearby."

"North of town." The change of subject had not sidetracked Peyton. "Michael's up there now with Casey Latimer. He's our part-time U.S. Marshal, occasional deputy, and husband to our local doctor."

Something in Peyton's voice had Wesley asking, "One of the women who terrify you?"

Peyton pursed his lips. "Emma Latimer, formerly of Boston. Emma, my wife, Briley, Hattie, and Clara are like sisters."

"Hattie White Eagle?"

"You've met her?"

Wesley shook his head. "Heard of her, or rather, heard her name in association with White Eagle Ranch."

"That's her. Carson, her husband, is as skilled a tracker as one can find in this territory. He may be of help."

"Find Hank before he finds them. Works for me." Wesley leaned against the chair back. "How far is his ranch?"

"Not too far, but he should be in town tomorrow. He and Hattie ride in two, three times a week."

"I'd appreciate it. I understand he doesn't need the work, but will he take it?"

"For pay?" Peyton shook his head. "No, but he'll do what he can to help. It's what we do here, and besides, you're a friend of Michael's."

Wesley lifted a single brow and cocked his head. He'd wager the sheriff heard his conversation with Clara and saw him give her the money. It was to the man's credit that he did not come out and say anything, and even more to his credit, he got his point across without nudging into Wesley's business. "Duly noted."

"What are you *not* telling me?"

"Plenty." Wesley bypassed the coffee in favor of finishing the water.

"Does Miss Tennyson know what you aren't telling me?" Peyton asked.

"Not enough for you to ask her." He leaned forward slightly and lowered his voice. "You'll get all you need from me, Sheriff. Later."

"All right." Peyton darted a glance toward the hall by the staircase. "How long were you a sharpshooter?"

His jaw tightened. "Too long." Wesley and Peyton stood simultaneously when Leah entered the dining room.

"Hello, gentlemen." Leah acknowledged Peyton before facing Wesley. "How long have you known I was listening?"

Wesley credited her with not denying it. Rather than answer her, he shrugged, though he recalled to the second when the fine hairs on his neck and arms raised from his heightened sense of her presence, and his heart pounded deeper in his chest. He attributed his years of sniper training to remaining calm and focused during Peyton's questioning.

Wesley pulled a chair out far enough for her to sit, and before he could help her scoot it closer to the table, Susan carried in a tray filled with the same offerings he'd receive, though in half the portions and with the addition of a cup of vegetable soup.

"Clara says you're to eat as much as you can." The cook efficiently cleared the other dishes from the table to the tray. "She's tending to something for her daughter, or she'd be here now."

Leah peered up at Susan and gave her a warm smile. "How old is her daughter?"

Susan beamed. "Alice is six, though she'll be seven soon enough. They grow so quickly. Now, you eat up, and then you'll have plenty of time to rest before dinner."

When Leah sat and stared at the food for a while after Susan left, Wesley prodded her by saying her name. She glanced up. "How does she think I can eat all this?"

The men smiled, and Peyton said, "Susan likes to feed people. Don't worry, she won't be insulted if you don't finish every bite." Peyton pushed his uneaten slice of pie toward Leah. "For dessert. I'll come back for more later."

When Leah dipped the silver spoon into the steaming broth and smoothly glided it over the back of the bowl before bringing it to her lips, Wesley forced himself to look away. He caught Peyton's raised brow and inquisitive smile but ignored both.

"Please, gentlemen, do not let my presence or my eating interfere with your conversation. If I recall, Sheriff Peyton, you inquired about what Mr. Davenport had not told me."

Peyton covered his mouth with his large hand to suppress a chuckle, then gave up and stood. "I'll return after you've rested, Miss Tennyson. Good luck, Wesley."

Leah stared after Peyton's retreating form, and once they were alone, she rested her spoon in the bowl. "Does he have no questions for me?"

"I'm sure he has a few."

"Regardless of the impression I gave, I was not listening for long."

Wesley knew precisely how long she listened. "I gave him

Hank's name and told him where I found you and how long we'd been together. The rest is for you to tell him—or not. It's up to you."

She closed her eyes and rubbed the bridge of her nose, trying to ease the tension churning beneath the skin. Leah no longer knew how to differentiate fear from worry or tiredness from defeat. She supposed only several hours of deep sleep would clear the fog of uncertain emotions roiling within. "What am I doing?"

Wesley caught her whispered words only because his focus never wavered from her. He pushed his coffee cup aside and leaned closer. "You're taking time."

Leah raised her eyes to meet his. "Time is a precious commodity, and I am certain I have depleted my store of it."

"If you think so, you're much more tired than I originally thought." He gently nudged her chin up with a finger. "You're still the same quick-thinking woman who protected Nelle, who kept you both alive for nearly a week in the wilderness, and who would have taken my life if necessary—or given yours." Wesley dropped his hand back to the table. "You and Nelle are the precious commodities. Time, we have plenty of, and that's a promise."

"You saved us out there, and I will never forget it, nor can I repay you."

Wesley longed to show her just how wrong she was, and though he refrained from leaning farther in and pulling her close, he indulged the impulse to run the back of his finger over her cheek. "You already have."

He didn't have to move his gaze away from Leah's face to know they were no longer alone. Wesley dropped his hand once more, pushed back the chair, and stood. "I'll leave you to finish your meal." He acknowledged Clara as the woman waited near the doorway holding an empty tray.

Leah caught his hand before he stepped away from the table. "Will you still be here when we wake up?"

"I'm not going anywhere." He rested his hand over hers. "Promise."

"You are rather free with your promises, Mr. Davenport."

"Wesley. When you know me better, Leah, you'll learn how wrong you are." He held Leah's eyes entranced for several seconds before breaking her temporary hold on him. Wesley smiled at Clara, excused himself, and retreated from the room, down the hall, and out the front door.

On the wide front porch of Clara Donaghue's impressive inn, Wesley inhaled the crisp air fragrant with pine and the spices he'd carried with him from the dining room. A punch to his midsection from a canon ball would not have startled him so severely as discovering that for the first time in his twenty-seven years, he'd met a woman possessing the power to claim his heart.

A TAP, TAP, TAP on the glass and the twittering singsong of morning birds awakened Leah from a sleep of such deep serenity it took her mind incremental stirrings to process her surroundings. How long had it been since her head rested on a plump down pillow or linens and quilts so fresh and warm cocooned her body? She longed to burrow deeper and ignore nature's urging for her to welcome the day.

Leah scrambled with the bed linens and pushed her torso upright. Seconds later, a conscious thought caught up with her brain and body working in sync. "It is all right. We're safe." Speaking the words aloud gave her the assurance not to panic.

She pushed off the quilts, swung her legs over the side of the bed, and nearly fell to the floor when her left leg twisted beneath her. Leah landed on one knee instead and braced her upper body on the mattress. "Graceful I am not."

When she extricated herself from the bedding and pushed her nightgown back down her legs, Leah found her footing and swept her pale-blond braid over her shoulder. Locating the robe Clara lent her, she left the room and went to Nelle's room next door. She'd wondered at the separate rooms, but Clara had assured her Nelle wouldn't be alone. Although five years younger, Clara's daughter, Allison, had championed Nelle and camped on the rug next to Nelle's bed.

The heavy meal from the late afternoon before, along with the distraction of her conversation with Wesley still flitting through her mind, stole away her strength to argue. Leah's trust in Clara had been absolute; otherwise, she never would have let Nelle from her sight.

"She's downstairs."

Leah clutched a hand over her pounding heart.

"I'm so sorry." Clara hurried to Leah's side. "I didn't mean to frighten you."

She had heard others describe having one's heart jump in one's chest, but she had never experienced it until now. "My thoughts overtook me, and I wasn't paying attention." Leah rubbed the hollow between her breasts to chase away the hammering in her chest. "Nelle is downstairs?"

Clara nodded, her countenance still etched with concern. "She's had her breakfast and is with Allison and Susan in the kitchen. My daughter has a fondness for assisting Susan when she's baking. There will be fresh scones for breakfast and an applesauce cake later to go with tea."

"I will dress then and join her." Leah, however, did not move. She pressed a hand to her stomach and braced her body against the wall. "Have you ever felt outside yourself looking in, unable to imagine what comes next?"

"Yes."

Leah's gaze flashed to Clara.

"Where were you during the war?"

The question caught Leah unawares, and she had to think back to three years before when her life had been on a different course. "I taught at a school for girls in Concord. Orphans mostly. We never heard the canon fire, and bodies never littered the landscape, but many from there lost someone."

"It was the same for me. We lived sheltered and unmolested by war, but it still touched the lives of our community. My mother and I used to visit a widow who had lost her husband, two sons, and a nephew during the first year of battles. I asked her a similar question when she received news of her second son's passing at Leesburg. It was an odd inquiry and one I had not considered much, but I recall her pouring tea right after she read the letter. A tear dripped from her eye, and she wiped it away before serving pound cake."

Leah choked back her own tears. "What did she say?"

"She quoted from scripture: 'My grace is all you need, for my power is the greatest when you are weak.' The widow had always been one for prayer and scripture, never without a bible, and never missing a Sunday service unless she was in service to others. I have never been more humbled than I was that day. I did not have her faith, but my lack led me to Crooked Creek, to a life with more love than I ever imagined possible."

Clara smiled and rested a hand on Leah's arm. "What comes next is a splash of water on your face, combing your hair, and dressing. After that, another step, then another. When you least expect it, you will see what comes next."

Survival necessitated every action she'd taken the past week, and Leah realized her mind and body still protected itself against unresolved threats. What if Wesley had not found them? The question prodded for an answer as she returned to her room, filled the porcelain bowl in the washstand, and splashed cool water on her face. She did not have a response by the time she pulled one of Clara's dresses over her head and slid it into place.

Struggling with the buttons up the back gave her more time to replay the moments she could remember after leaving Hank Duggan's camp. She possessed no skill for covering tracks or misdirection, and more than once she'd noticed a tear or missing piece of fabric from hers or Nelle's skirts, no doubt hanging like a tattered breadcrumb upon a gnarled twig. How had Hank not found them?

The question remained when Leah descended the steps, then temporarily retreated at the sound of Nelle's sweet laughter.

"Leah?"

She turned and smiled at Clara. "I'm all of a piece now."

Clara returned the smiled. "Susan has a plate warming for you if you're ready for breakfast."

"Do you have no other guests?"

"Two left this morning. Summer is busier, but I enjoy the quiet months of winter and early spring."

It was on Leah's tongue to ask why a wealthy woman from Connecticut ran a small hotel in the mountain territory. She refrained and considered Clara's comment about breakfast. Prudence bid her to wait, for a full stomach did not go well with the conversation she needed to have with the sheriff. "Perhaps later, if that is all right. I should like to find Sheriff Sawyer first."

Clara's smile softened to one of compassion. "He is already here, in the parlor with Mr. Davenport."

The tremble in her fingers and lips served as a further reminder that she was not on holiday in a quiet town surrounded by mountains so high they appeared to reach the heavens and forests so thick they blanketed the landscape. Fear brought her and Nelle to Crooked Creek, and she hoped Wesley was right to place his trust in the sheriff and U.S. Marshal.

She held fast to the silent prayer in her heart that she, too, could trust these men to put rightness before the rule of law.

Leah faced the direction of the parlor when the sweet laughter once again drifted from the kitchen.

"Come along." Clara motioned for her to follow, and Leah did, through the double doors to an alcove abutting the kitchen. They remained there, looking in on the giggling girls holding up flour-covered hands. Evidence of flour streaks remained on

Nelle and Allison's faces. Susan held her hands at her hips, but her tightened mouth indicated someone trying to keep from smiling. Susan waggled a finger at each of them before digging her hands back into a bowl of dough, all the while chuckling and shaking her head. "All right, you two, back to the baking, or we'll have no pies today."

Leah backed out of the kitchen and into the dining room. Clara followed.

"She is so happy. It's difficult to believe now that only yesterday we were—" Leah glanced over her shoulder toward the parlor. "I should get on."

"You were what?" Clara asked.

Leah shook her head. "Perhaps later we can visit?"

"Of course."

Girding herself for what lay ahead, Leah left Clara's comforting presence. Upon entering the parlor, Wesley and Peyton stood, and Leah realized that comfort emanated from both men. "Gentlemen."

"Miss Tennyson."

Peyton held out his hand for her to accept first. His gentle grip offered warmth without pressure. "Sheriff Peyton. Thank you for returning."

"Nothing is more important right now than helping you and Nelle."

The skin around the edge of Peyton's eyes crinkled when he smiled, a testament to many moments of laughter that she imagined enriched his life. Leah drew comfort from the simple detail and trusted this man all the more for it.

With only some conscious thought, Leah filled the space on the settee next to Wesley. Neither scooted away from the other when Wesley sat straighter, and his arm brushed against hers. The security of his closeness slowed her thudding heartbeats. "His name is Hank Duggan."

Neither man responded to her unexpected whisper, and for a few seconds, she wondered if they had heard her. She barely recognized the softly spoken words as her own, but when Peyton nodded, a slow up and down that put Leah in mind of a man buying time to think.

She opened her hands and released the skirt fabric she'd unconsciously scrunched into her fists. Smoothing the material, she looked directly at the sheriff. "I will not give her back to them, Sheriff Peyton, and the badge you wear will not change my mind or my intentions."

The weight of Wesley's hand pressed on her shoulder before gliding down her arm to cover her hand. No words could have bolstered her strength as much as the gentle and reassuring touch.

"First, Miss Tennyson, I have no intention of doing anything until I hear the whole of what you have to say. And I mean *all* of it." He narrowed his eyes a little and tilted his head forward until she nodded in understanding. "Good. Now, Wesley didn't tell me much, but what he did reassured me that you've done right by Nelle. A child's trust is about the toughest to gain and the easiest to lose, so I already know enough not to act rashly. Having said that, there is the law to consider—" He held up a hand to ward off any protests from her lips. "And the law makes allowances for what is right. At least where I'm concerned it does. My interest right now is to remove any threat against Nelle. Then we'll deal with the knot you've woven yourself into regarding the girl's custody."

Leah blew out a quick breath of relief, though the constriction around her heart had only eased a little. "Thank you. I can give you a fair description of Mr. Duggan. The man Wesley waylaid on our behalf confirmed it was not him."

Peyton's mouth set in a straight line. "Waylaid is a delicate way of putting it, Miss Tennyson, and you don't need to worry about him. There's every chance that man simply saw an opportunity and meant to take advantage."

Leah's glance strayed to Wesley, who she found studying her. The intensity of his gaze forced her to turn back to Peyton. She knew not what she glimpsed in his eyes, but she recognized her own inability to deal with it, at least until she'd built up the right defenses.

"I can sketch this Hank Duggan while Miss Tennyson describes him." Both Peyton and Leah turned toward Wesley. He shrugged. "It passes the time."

Peyton nodded. "All right. I'd appreciate the help. Now, Miss Tennyson."

"Please, call me Leah."

"Leah. How long were you and Nelle with the Duggans? Wesley was short on those details."

"Do not scold him, Sheriff, for I have not told him the whole of it yet. Two and a half months, to answer your question." Leah leaned backward a little to rest against the cushion. She kept her hand beneath Wesley's. "In Missouri, we joined a train of thirteen wagons heading to Oregon and stayed with them until Casper. It was a relatively uneventful journey, and Nelle enjoyed the company of the other children."

"What happened at Casper?"

"Three wagons broke off the company to head north. The others were going to a place called Diamond City near Confederate Gulch. Hank Duggan said he had a stake in a mine at a place called Bannack."

Peyton leaned forward and rubbed his palms together in a sawing motion twice. "Both those places are a long way from Crooked Creek. You would have been traveling with the Duggans for two or three weeks before you reached Bannack. How long were you two by yourselves in the wilderness?"

"Five, perhaps six days before Wesley found us. I counted, but the last day or two when we, that is I . . ."

"No need to explain." Peyton sat straight and brought his long legs forward in preparation to stand. "That's enough for now. If you're up to it, I'd like Wesley to work up the sketch of Duggan."

When Peyton stood, Leah automatically rose. She noticed

Wesley reached full height right when she did, with his hand cupping her elbow. "That's all?"

Peyton squeezed her hands once before releasing them, and his mouth curved upward on one side. "I can come up with a dozen more questions if you'd like, but it won't be necessary. The sketch will do for now. Based on the information you've provided, we can estimate where you departed ways with Duggan."

Leah stepped toward him half a foot. "You will find him, won't you? I wondered, many times, and still do, why he hadn't found us yet. Nelle and I did not move quickly, especially since I didn't know where were going."

Wesley met Peyton's curious glance. "As it happens, we wondered the same thing."

THE DELICATE SKIN ABOVE her eyes remained motionless while beneath them, her gently rounded nose twitched once. She brushed her finger across the top and stilled again. Soft lips moved—no, glided—open and closed with every word of description she relayed to Wesley. Her narrow neck disappeared beneath the lace-edged dress collar. Wesley's fingers itched to sketch her instead, so he pulled his gaze from Leah's face and returned his focus to the drawing.

Hank Duggan put Wesley in mind of the word "medium." As Leah once told him, nothing about him stood out as exceptional, but neither did he lack all the features a woman might find handsome.

"I think that's it."

Wesley added a little more shadow around Duggan's eyes, mostly because it added a hollowness he suspected Leah might recognize. "I think so." He waited three counts until she opened one eye, then the other. "Are you sure you want to look at this?"

"No, not at all."

He kept the sketch side facing him while she decided.

"All right. You can show me."

Wesley took his time about it. "He's just as you described—average. Unimpressive, even." He turned the sheet of paper over to reveal the result of his labors and her description.

"Oh, my."

Leah reached toward it and then yanked her fingers back. "You do yourself a disservice to call your talent a mere hobby. The only place you will find a better likeness is on Hank Duggan's face. It is his very image. Even around the eyes. I remember they did not look so hallow or shadowed when I first met him."

"Did his wife give birth on the trail?"

"Yes, in Casper. The baby did not survive the birth. It was a boy."

Wesley turned the sketch back toward him and studied the face. "I'm sorry for his wife, then."

Leah nodded. "Her name is Maeve, and she was kind to us both, though quieter after she buried her son. Such trials make a person long to return to the comfort of home."

"Is that what you wanted?" *Or want*, he added silently.

"Frankly, I know not what I want beyond keeping Nelle safe." Leah rolled her shoulders back, rose from the settee, and walked to the window. "There is nothing left for me in Massachusetts."

Wesley waited for the catch in her voice to hint of sadness, but it never came. He joined her at the window, where beyond the glass panes and the welcoming front porch, tree branches with spring leaves fluttered in the breeze. Two chickadees danced a fluttering circle in the air before swooping beyond their sight.

He stood as close to her as possible without entering her personal space uninvited. To his immense relief, she made the first half circle to face him. "There's a new beginning for everyone somewhere, Leah."

"And where is your beginning?"

"Here, I hope." Wesley spoke the truth, if not the whole of it.

"When this is over . . ."

He brushed his fingers up her arm and rested his palms on her shoulders. "Yes?"

"You won't . . . I mean, will you—"

The front door on the other side of the parlor wall rattled open with unexpected force, bringing heavy thuds from boots with it. They paused their words, movements, and even their breath as they stared at each other and waited for the inevitable interruption.

"Is he here?"

Wesley recognized the voice, even after the years since he last spoke with Michael Donaghue.

Clara's voice reached them next. "He is, but busy now."

"You should go." Leah gripped his forearm, but she held fast rather than tugging his hand from her shoulder. "None of this is going to be easy, is it?" she whispered.

Wesley cursed his old friend's timing and closed his eyes before pressing his forehead against Leah's. "Not all of it." His heart, mind, and body each raged a different battle inside him, for none could agree on the best course. Wesley's practical reason won for the moment, and he eased away without putting distance between them. "Come, I want you to meet Michael."

Leah nodded, saying nothing. He gave them both another minute to regain balance before clasping her hand and urging her to join him. They stopped beneath the arch to the parlor. Their sudden appearance halted the muted conversation between husband and wife.

Wesley couldn't guess who grinned at whom first, but he'd call it a draw. He released Leah's hand long enough to meet Michael's halfway for a back-pounding embrace.

"I never thought I'd see you again." Michael Donaghue, comrade and friend, gave Wesley one last friendly smack on his shoulder before pulling away and slipping an arm around his wife's waist. "Peyton caught me in town on my way home. I had to see for myself that Wesley Davenport was in Crooked Creek."

"There's a little mystery we need to clear up, but that can wait." Wesley stepped back to Leah's side. "Miss Leah Tennyson, I'd like you to meet Clara's husband, Michael Donaghue."

"A genuine pleasure, Mr. Donaghue. I have heard wonderful things about you, and your wife has been a saving grace."

Michael kissed Clara's cheek. "It is one of her many gifts." His smile softened, then faded away. "Peyton also explained some of what has brought you here, Miss Tennyson."

"Please, I give you leave to call me, Leah. Without Wesley, we would not have made it this far." Leah tugged on Wesley's arm to draw his attention. "You and Michael should catch up. I want to look in on Nelle."

Wesley didn't want to let her go from his sight, let alone from his side. "We'll talk?"

Leah nodded. "Yes, later." Mindful of their company, she said nothing more about it.

Clara brushed a kiss over her husband's mouth, then motioned for Leah to follow her. "Let us see what our girls are into, and I smell lemon cake, so the kitchen is the best place to visit right now." Clara looped her arm through Leah's. "And if they behave themselves, the gentlemen can enjoy a slice after Michael has freshened up."

When they were left alone, Wesley released a breath and rubbed both hands over his face.

"How deep are you in?"

He didn't pretend not to know what Michael meant. "All the way. You can't imagine what it's—" Wesley caught Michael's raised brow. "Yes, you can imagine. I'm happy for you—you and Clara. She's a prize, which begs me to ask how you convinced her to marry you?"

"Are you looking for advice?"

Wesley watched the hallway the women had disappeared down minutes before.

"Whoa. You're well and truly in deep, aren't you. It's the real thing."

"As real as it gets for me." Before embarrassing them with emotions he had no experience in sharing, Wesley slapped his friend on the shoulder. "You can freshen up, as your wife put it, or we can sit on the front porch, and you can explain the bank draft."

"That's what brought you here?"

Wesley nodded. "For starters."

Without verbal agreement, they moved their conversation from the foyer to Clara's front porch. Once comfortable in two generously sized wooden chairs, Wesley spoke first. "I'm listening."

"You really don't remember?"

Wesley stretched a leg out in front of him. "I remember a lot of things about the war, but not a single event comes to mind explaining why you think you owe me eight hundred dollars."

"Isaac Worth."

"I remember him. We'll get to how you know him in a minute." Wesley pulled back his leg and leaned forward a few inches.

"And?"

"And, Michael, I'm trying to decide if I want to hit you until sense rattles around in your brain."

"Which is why I mailed the draft instead of delivering it myself." Michael waggled his finger between them. "To avoid just that end. Clara likes my face the way it is. Besides, you might think differently when I tell you the debt isn't mine, nor is the money."

Wesley stilled. "Explain, please."

"It's too long of a story to replay it in full right now, but the short of it is, Isaac traveled with me two and half years ago when I came searching for my sister. A lot happened, and some of it reminded me too much of the war, but I got Clara and Alice out of it so I'd do it all over again. I digress. Clara and I ended up buying a lumber mill north of here. We gave Isaac a small share to help him start his new life. He would have turned it down if we hadn't agreed to put an end date of three years on it."

Wesley's head swirled with thoughts from around the time he had met Isaac Worth. "Why did you send it?"

"Isaac wrote a year ago asking for the last eight hundred dollars of his profits to be sent to you instead."

"Where is Isaac now?"

"He returned to North Carolina with a woman he helped save here. They've built a good life for themselves, have two children. They're not without struggles, but they don't want to live anywhere else." Michael chuckled and added, "I think the weather also decided it for him. Too cold, too much snow, and during the winter, the sun hides behind clouds more than half the days."

"Sounds like paradise."

"It can be."

Wesley heard the seriousness behind Michael's light tone and responded in kind. "Isaac didn't owe me anything. How in the hell did you meet him anyway?"

"The war shrunk the country far more than any of us realized." Michael readjusted his seat in the chair and rested his head against the back. "Isaac shared more stories on the journey to Montana than I can recall, but your name came up in one of mine and one of his."

"Did you meet him before or after I did?"

"After. Although, Isaac never explained how he knew you until he wrote me last year. You're the one who gave the doctor the money to buy him so he could free him and teach him his trade."

Though he said it matter-of-factly, Wesley heard the appreciation in Michael's words.

"You saved him, and he saved me. Had he told me sooner, I would have repaid you myself, but it was important to Isaac to do it this way."

Wesley thought of the money now in the way Isaac had intended, and although he didn't need it or want it, neither could he return it, knowing why it mattered.

"And now you're here. Could be Isaac had more than one plan when he asked me to send the draft on his behalf. This is a good place to start fresh."

"I'm glad to hear Isaac's doing well and is happy." With the issue of the money settled, Wesley now had to decide what to do with it. He didn't want to think about it right now. What Wesley wanted more than his next breath was to look upon Leah's face again. "How much did the sheriff tell you about Leah?"

"Everything he knows so far. Peyton wanted me to know the situation so I can help you watch for anyone suspicious. We'll close the inn to guests until the situation resolves, unless it's women and children who show up. Nothing will convince Clara to turn them away. It's a slow time of year, which will help. What can I do to help Leah?"

The sturdy railing beckoned Wesley to stand and stretch his legs, so he did, and when he rested again, he sat on the edge of a handrail. "I don't want to leave her while I go out there, but I need to look for this Duggan person."

"Peyton and Casey Latimer—our part-time territorial marshal—are handling the search. Casey is heading out to the White Eagle Ranch to speak with Carson. There's no better tracker." Michael paused a beat. "Except maybe you. How much did you tell Peyton about yourself?"

"Your sheriff saw the Whitworth and assumed a lot from there. Some of it's probably accurate." Wesley tapped a staccato against the wood with a finger. "You don't even know the whole of it, Michael."

"Peyton probably expects you to head out yourself. Any of us would do the same to keep the women we care about safe."

Wesley obsessed over every scenario and asked himself if it had to be him who tracked Hank Duggan, or if he could trust it to someone else to see the job done. Reining in and isolating his emotions for Leah only stifled his instincts. "None of this is going to be easy, is it?" He repeated her question in a silent loop and realized she was right.

"Do you know if the marshal has already left?"

Michael nodded. "He'll speak with you first, before they do anything. It will be dark by the time Casey returns from the ranch, so there's nothing to be done tonight. Carson will show up in the morning."

Wesley gripped the railing's edge until he felt his knuckles numb. Blood rushed through the limbs when he released the wood and spread his fingers. "Did you tell Clara everything?"

"Everything important, and then some." Michael finally stood, shaking the dust from his jacket that he'd been carrying since he returned home an hour ago. "I'm going to freshen up as my wife suggested, then enjoy a slice of the lemon cake. Susan is a wonder in the kitchen."

"So I've heard." Wesley smiled. "I've already sampled some of her cooking and look forward to more."

"Then go find Leah. Tell her what you need to. We'll have tea soon and dinner a few hours later with light conversation, then you can rest well tonight. You'll have a clearer head come morning." Michael stopped at the door, ready to turn the handle. "And if you ride out tomorrow, I promise Leah and Nelle will be safe. Ellis, Susan's husband, is always around, and I won't go anywhere while you're gone. The folks in this town look after each other."

Wesley remained on the porch long after Michael left him alone. He tried to distinguish one sound from the next, separate rustling leaves from chirping birds. Only when a high-pitched series of whistles and piping sounded from above did Wesley's thoughts break their reverie. He left the porch for the soft grass immediately in front of the inn, then walked out farther to peer beyond its rooftop and the shading trees.

High in the pale blue sky mottled with white-and-gray clouds, a pair of eagles swooped past each other only to return, circle, and soar higher still until it appeared their wing tips caressed a cloud. A soft call, unlike any sound Wesley had ever heard, joined the whistles and pipes, until the eagles came together, talons locked, and circled to earth. He watched them release and part close to the earth, only to soar once again into the sky and disappear from view.

"It is their courtship dance."

Wesley relaxed and walked to her. Leah stood a dozen feet away, her cheeks pink from the cool afternoon. Her eyes drew their color from the gray wool shawl wrapped over her shoulders and around her torso. "How long have you been outside?"

"Almost as long as you were with Michael. Nelle and Alice were learning to bake from Susan, and Clara suggested fresh air. She was right."

He couldn't stop a slight frown from forming. "You're alone?"

Leah reached up and lifted the edges of his mouth with two fingers. "That's better. Clara walked with me for a bit, and when she realized I wanted some time alone, she suggested I stay close to the house."

"Show me."

Leah slanted her head to the side as though weighing her choices. In response, she accepted his outstretched hand and led him around to the rear of the inn where light-green grass and glacier lilies covered a mini meadow that spanned the space between the inn, a thick wood, and a small log cabin beyond.

"It's quiet."

"The quiet is soothing, is it not?"

Wesley recalled moments during the war when he longed for

nothing more than silence. At other times, the stillness served as a harbinger of battles ahead. "Leah—"

"Do not say it, please. Not yet."

He took two steps in a half circle to face her. "Don't say what?"

"You are leaving."

Wesley lefted her chin with the tip of his thumb. "How could you think I'd ever leave you when all I want to do is keep you close?" He brushed her lips with his own, surprising them both without warning. The gentle caress deepened beyond what even his imagination had hoped for, her arms winding around his neck as their mouths moved together in harmony. Wesley gathered her close, unwilling to allow even a whisper of space between them.

He struggled for air, yet decided sacrificing his breath was worth every stroke of her soft lips and whimpers. He regained enough self-control to fight the sudden lightheadedness and remember his parents raised a gentleman. When they finally parted, Leah's arms remained around his neck, and he gave them the extra time to steady themselves.

Leah's weakened arms released their hold and fell to her sides. Wesley's remained at her waist until they traveled a path upward until he held her face in the cradle of his hands. "I'm not leaving you, but I *am* going after Duggan."

She gripped his arms. "Why does it have to be you?"

He prayed his eyes conveyed what he could not yet say in words. Three days he'd known her, yet he had not needed even half that time to recognize the overwhelming pressure in his chest as proof.

"Please, continue to trust me, Leah."

He rode out the following morning at dawn while the pinks and reds of sunrise waited for their turn to herald in the new day. Casey Latimer and Carson White Eagle rode with him, flanked on either side, yet slightly behind, giving Wesley the lead. Somehow, they understood it mattered to him.

"They know what they're doing," Clara said from behind her.

Leah had not heard her come onto the porch. When she peered over her shoulder, she saw Michael had also joined her. "I believe they do, but as we know, even the strongest and most skilled of men don't always return."

"Wesley's more skilled than most." Michael stood to her right, and Clara beside him.

"You fought alongside him?"

Michael nodded. "A few times. Our assignments aligned for a period near the war's start."

"And what did he do during these assignments?"

When Michael answered her question with silence, Leah said, "You cannot or will not tell me. It is all right. Do not think I am upset or feel it is my right to hear what Wesley has not told me himself. I have no claim to his past, and he has asked for my trust."

Leah clutched a fist to her breast. "Why then can I not take a full breath without this unbearable pain searing through me?"

Michael quietly left them alone. Instead of Wesley's arms embracing her, Clara stood at her side and held her close as they both stared at the empty road.

"He said it had to be him."

"Perhaps it did." Clara released her and leaned against a porch post. "I met Michael standing on this porch early one morning. I still remember the red, yellow, and orange hues fading from one shade to the next. Winter's cold already blanketed the valley, and I wore only a shawl and blanket for protection, but I came out here as I often do to read before the day begins. He rode up to the porch, and I knew my life would never be the same. It took me a while to understand why, but my heart recognized him."

Leah understood with frightening clarity what Clara meant. "And so it had to be him."

"Yes, and it was. Michael saved my life and has saved it every day since simply by loving me. It is in their nature, Leah, and surrendering our safety to a man does not make us weak, for through their strength we become stronger."

"You speak of love, and I can imagine it, but it is not that way with me and Wesley."

Clara smiled, though Leah did not see the slight curve of her mouth. "Perhaps not, but whatever is between you, give it the opportunity to strengthen you. You will need all your strength for what you are about to face."

Leah raised a delicately arched brow. "What am I about to face?"

Clara pointed toward the road. "Emma, Hattie, and Briley."

"They do not look terrifying." Leah squinted her eyes a little until the three women walked closer, their smiles evident as they talked among themselves.

Clara surprised her with a burst of laughter. "Our husbands call us terrifying and are not afraid to admit it. No, what you are about to face is not at all terrifying."

"Then why—"

"You will see." Clara hugged her once and moved away to descend the steps and greet her friends.

Leah stayed on the porch, her eyes roving over each woman as they approached. She studied their clothing, facial expressions, and how they carried themselves, and the similarity became obvious when Clara joined them. Each of them possessed their own unique beauty, and not one resembled the other, yet Leah would swear to their sisterhood. She'd never known such a bond.

"Leah!" Nelle bounded through the open front doors seconds before the four women ascended the porch steps. "Miss Susan said I can go to the market with her and Alice if you give your permission."

Alice rushed to join her new friend. "Please, Miss Leah! May Nelle go with us?" Alice turned to her mother. "We promise to be careful."

Clara smoothed an errant lock of her daughter's fair hair. "Does Susan know you are out here?"

Alice considered her mother's question and gave her an indirect answer. "She said we had to ask Miss Leah."

Leah looked first to Clara.

"The general store is not far, and I will ask Michael to go with them."

A blush warmed Leah's neck at their audience and her overprotectiveness. "You may go, Nelle, but stay close to Susan. It looks like it might rain, so be sure to wear . . ." Leah realized Nelle did not have a coat or hat except the ones she wore on the trail.

"Yes," Clara said with a quick glance and a reassuring smile to Leah. "Nelle's bonnet and shawl are on the hook by the back door. Alice knows where we keep the parasols and umbrellas."

The girls skipped back into the house and called out to Susan on their way to the kitchen, leaving Leah overwhelmed in the company of Clara and three strangers.

"Hattie's son and mine still have a few years to go before they catch up with Alice. It's nice to see her have a friend under the same roof again." The woman with coppery-red hair and striking blue eyes stepped forward and held out her hand to Leah. "I'm Emma Latimer. Welcome to Crooked Creek."

DAMP EARTH AND THE surrounding mist from the gentle rain slowed their ride two hours outside town. When they had departed the inn this morning, his riding companions may have expected to travel for at least two or three days. Wesley, however, did not expect to travel far. If Duggan wanted Nelle as much as

Leah suspected—and he trusted Leah's instincts—then Duggan would be close.

Wesley had still not worked out how Leah and Nelle put enough distance between them and Duggan to manage their escape. He held up a fist and stopped his horse. He pointed toward the tree to their right and motioned for Carson and Casey to advance from the north and south. Wesley assumed both men agreed when he left the road for the trees. He dismounted Revere just inside the tree line, wrapped the reins loosely around the saddle horn, and left the animal to graze.

On silent tread, Wesley moved through the trees toward the sappy scent of green, damp wood burning in a campfire. Too much smoke billowed upward, creating a thick soot trail in the mist.

Three men huddled around the fire, their voices too low to carry. One had their back to Wesley, another showed his profile, and the third . . . he's the one Wesley most wanted. The Hank Duggan of Leah's recollection sat facing Wesley, his entire attention devoted to the spit-roasted bird he was turning. Now and then, he looked up from his task to say something to one of his companions. Unaware of Wesley's presence, Duggan removed the bird from the smoky fire and tore off the first piece of meat before passing it around.

He needed—no, wanted—to be on the other side of the men, at Duggan's back. Wesley wondered how tolerant the marshal would be of a more permanent reckoning than sending Duggan to the territorial prison. Harboring no confidence to such an end, Wesley hoped Duggan gave him no other choice.

Skirting around the campfire took several minutes and careful stepping. When Wesley reached the other side, he saw Casey far enough away to go unnoticed yet close enough to aid within seconds. Carson remained hidden, which did not surprise him, considering Michael's description of the man's skill on the battlefield.

Wesley trusted the other two men to be where he needed

them at the right time. He approached Duggan from behind, his Wentworth steady in his arms. "There's nowhere to go."

The three men around the campfire stilled until the biggest among them reached for his sidearm. A shot rang out through the trees from Casey's direction and caught the man in the shoulder. His scream rent the air, and he tumbled off his stone perch, clutching at his wounded arm.

"The next one goes in your head, Duggan. Remove your gun and toss it as far away into the trees as far as you can."

"Who the hell are you?"

"Five seconds, both of you."

The shorter man sitting next to Duggan tossed his pistol first and held up his hands.

"What do you think you're doing?" Duggan punched the other man's side.

"You aren't paying us enough to get killed." Duggan's companion, gaunt of face and slender of build, slowly stood. "Mind if I step out of the crosshairs?"

"I do." Wesley motioned with his rifle for the man to sit back down. "Your turn, Duggan."

He tossed his pistol to the other side of the campfire, close enough for his friend to jump and reach for it if the chance arose. Casey emerged from hiding and gathered the weapons.

"Just the two of you?" Duggan spit onto the ground. "You'll regret this."

Casey pulled back the edge of his coat to reveal the silver U.S. Marshal badge. "Your indignation is understandable, but any regret will be yours if you don't listen to the man behind you."

"He a marshal, too?"

"More like a man out for revenge."

Duggan held up his arms and twisted his body to get a look at Wesley. "I don't know you."

"Not yet."

Carson chose that moment to join them. He carried two

thin ropes, and without saying a word, tied Duggan's hands together, then secured his arms against his back by wrapping more rope around his torso. He did the same to the other two men, taking an extra minute to press a cloth to the bleeding man's wound before crouching next to the stone circle and tossing clumps of damp dirt on the fire. The flames hissed and spurted as Carson smothered them. He picked up a hot stone from the circle and held it over the wounded man. "It will stop the bleeding."

"You stay away from me, you crazy half-breed!"

Duggan's eyes narrowed. "What do you mean half-breed, Jake?"

"I seen this crazy man before. White something is his name. Crazy as any—owww!"

Carson pressed his soft boot on the man's shoulder and dropped the stone. "Better?" Without asking for direction, Carson yanked the smaller man to his feet and steadied him before giving Duggan the same treatment. "Start walking."

"We can't walk like this!" Duggan shouted.

"Figure it out." Carson pointed behind Wesley. "Their horses are not far."

"What about me?" The wounded man on the ground rolled, cried out in pain, and ended up on his back.

Carson helped him to his feet. "Be grateful he didn't shoot your leg. Now, walk."

Wesley watched the scene play out, Carson and Casey in tandem, each of them obviously used to working with the other. His attention never left Duggan, though. At full height, even with his hands tied behind his back, the man stood barely an inch shorter than Wesley. His sheer size would have overpowered Leah and Nelle if given the chance. How did they get away? "I need a few minutes alone with him."

Duggan's rapid headshake left Casey unmoved. "Ten minutes."

"You can't do this! You're the law!" The shouts gained no sympathy.

Wesley circled, his rifle lowered, until he faced Duggan. "Where's your wife?"

Duggan's eyes widened. "Who the hell are you? How do you know about Maeve?"

"Answer the question."

His jaw, tight and tense, loosened only when Wesley nudged him with the rifle muzzle. "Trading post."

"Where are you headed?" When he remained silent, Wesley pushed him down on the nearest log.

"The next town. For supplies."

Wesley sighed and crouched, putting him at eye level with Duggan. "Nelle Martin."

The intense stare Duggan focused on Wesley might have scared another man into submission. Wesley had seen worse, survived worse, and sometimes to his regret, meted out worse than the anger and violence he saw in Duggan's eyes.

"You're the one who took them?"

"Why not give up?" Wesley asked, instead of answering. "They got away and you could have joined them. I might have still come after you, but you've made it easier. Why?"

Duggan tightened his lips and looked at the ground. Wesley responded by shoving off the man's hat and yanking his head back by his scruffy hair. The man howled, then grit his teeth. "I'll give you half. Hell, I'll give you all the money."

Wesley delivered a blow to Duggan's midsection that contracted his stomach, forcing a painful breath from his body. "You sold her."

"She's a prime piece. I'd rather get between Leah's—"

The next blow landed across Duggan's face. "To whom?"

"You're getting nothing from me." Duggan spit blood on the ground, barely missing Wesley's boot. "Nothing."

"We'll see about that." Wesley's stomach roiled, and his chest burned with anger, and he was out of time. He jerked

Duggan to his feet and pushed him in the direction of the horses.

By the time they reached the others, Carson and Casey had managed to get Duggan's riding companions onto the back of their horses, where they sat precariously in their saddles. When Wesley shoved the man forward, Casey stepped forward to help Duggan onto his horse. He wanted to put his hands around Duggan's neck and choke both truth and life from him. Having to face Leah after committing such an act is all that stopped him.

She shined through the darkness of his life, a beacon of hope, a reminder of all that was still good in the world. He wanted to be a source of that good for her. His heart tripped several beats and took a few moments to steady itself before calming down.

With Carson's help, he got Duggan in his saddle. "Don't try to cause trouble and you might stay in your seat." Wesley pulled himself onto Revere's back and gave Casey a steady look. "Marshal."

Casey gave Wesley a single nod. "We have them."

Wesley left Hank and the others to Carson and the marshal while he rode ahead. With the rain stopped and the road into town dry enough in spots not to impede travel, Wesley spurred Revere into a run, giving the animal its head.

"Keep your heels down a bit more. That's right. Now, loosen your grip a little on the reins. She's not going anywhere without you."

"I'm riding, Leah!"

Leah's smile matched Nelle's. The young girl rode in a circle while Hattie held a longer leather lead and walked a few paces ahead of her mare. Hattie White Eagle, the woman with emerald eyes and flaxen hair barely a shade darker than Clara's, winked at Clara, but said to Nelle, "You'll be jumping fences in no time."

"Please, no." Leah laid a flat hand over her heart, though not at the thought of Nelle learning to ride a horse with Hattie's skill. Will Nelle be with me long enough to learn all about horses? Or to watch eagles soar below a summer sun or stroll across meadows deep in summer grass? Leah's mind held only a dearth of answers accompanied by too many questions.

"No one is better with horses than Hattie, except maybe her husband. You've nothing to fear, Leah. Relax."

Leah met Briley Sawyer's honey-brown eyes and immediately saw the resemblance to Michael Donaghue. She saw why the sheriff had been drawn to the pretty Irish woman whose voice echoed the faraway land's lyrical music. Briley had misinterpreted Leah's fright, which Leah thought best.

"They have been gone for several hours now."

Briley's sympathetic smile conveyed both empathy and hope. "Casey and Carson know the land from here to the surrounding territories, and from what my brother has told me of Wesley . . . well, I expect he's as safe as can be."

"Of course, you are right. I seem to fret over everything of late."

"It is to be expected, with what you've been through." Briley leaned against the base of a stalwart oak behind the inn where Hattie was giving Nelle her impromptu riding lesson. "Most of us are not like Hattie, living like she was born to this wild land. Emma perhaps is the closest, for she had seen much of illness and death before she came here. Clara had this grand home waiting her arrival.

"Me, I would not have survived without the love and friendship of these women and the people of this town gave me when I first arrived. Peyton tells me differently, but I know the truth. I learned it was okay to accept help, for help given in love is not charity. You'll work hard if you stay, Leah. Everyone who lives in this place, no matter their station or wealth, must learn to work hard if they want to survive, and oh, it is so worth the effort when surviving becomes thriving."

Leah could imagine herself living in such a place. Mountains that offered as much protection as danger, valleys wide and resplendent with grass enough for grazing and space enough to never worry if the world was closing in. "I do not know where I will be tomorrow. Nelle's safety comes first, and then I must answer for what I've done."

"What have you done, Leah, except keep that girl safe?" Emma stood on the back porch, her exit from the house and presence behind them having gone unnoticed.

"The law—"

"Is not as black and white as you might think, especially out here." Emma walked down the steps and waved to Nelle, who beamed and begged Hattie to go faster. "What could anyone expect the law in this land to do except protect the woman whose only crime is to save a young girl?"

Leah understood the question to be rhetorical, and the answer came without prompting. "I have not secured her safety yet."

Emma looped an arm through Leah's and pointed to Nelle. "Well, you must be looking at something different than I am right now."

The back door slapped against its wood frame when Clara hurried onto the back porch. "Wesley is riding up."

Leah didn't want to see Duggan again.

"He's alone."

Lifting the hem of her skirt so the fabric wouldn't catch beneath her feet, Leah set a brisk pace, just shy of a run, her shawl slipping down her arms. Uncertain how she came to be at the front of the inn so quickly, she said nothing before Wesley brought her close and breathed deeply against her hair. "I needed to hold you."

As far as expected explanations, his muffled words held no

relation to any that came to mind. Leah cared only that he not let go. "Did you find him?"

She felt his response against her head and could not stop a shudder. "Where is he?"

Wesley leaned back and cupped her face. "You won't have to see him."

"Except I do. I need him to tell me why. He has a wife who loves him. What made him choose to act with such evil in his heart? I know what he intended. I'm not wrong about what he planned."

"No, you're not." Wesley kissed her forehead. "But you may have been wrong about his intentions, and it may not be only him."

Leah's heart misstepped, her mind racing with all the possibilities of what Wesley might say next. "What do you mean?"

"Duggan was with two other men. They seemed to know each other well enough, but I doubt Duggan is paying them, and they aren't the sort who would work for free."

"The Duggans had enough money to reach Montana, but Hank was counting on finding work right away in the mines." Leah stepped back and rubbed her arms. "At least, he said as much to me. My instincts must have failed."

"Your instincts saved Nelle. You can berate yourself if it eases your mind, but it won't help you or the girl. If you want to speak to Duggan, it won't be alone."

Leah's brow furrowed in thought. "I agree, though I prefer it to be only the two of us first, if the sheriff and marshal will allow it."

"They will."

"You sound confident." A slight movement drew Leah's gaze past Wesley's arm to the front window closest to them. Nelle and Allison's angelic faces pressed against the glass. "Nelle has an aunt somewhere in Oregon, Nelle thinks."

Wesley's brow raised as he turned to see what held Leah's focus. "We're not alone."

"She is curious and hesitant to ask about anything beyond a single moment."

"Why did the aunt not take Nelle in?"

Leah angled herself to smile at Nelle and spoke to Wesley in a quieter tone. "Nelle mentioned her aunt, a woman she has not met, on the train journey west. The orphanage attempted to locate her, but without a place to start, their inquiries went unanswered. Oregon is what Nelle's father had told her about before he died. It is his wife's sister."

"Oregon Territory was vast, but it's been broken off now, with Oregon now part of the Union and Washington and Idaho are their own territories. If her aunt was in Oregon Territory back then, she could be——"

"Anywhere."

"If you want us to find her, we will. Casey will have connections with marshals in nearby territories, and an old army commander of mine has been in Boise since they built a fort there in '63. He wrote me before I came west, so he's likely still in Idaho." Wesley shrugged. "We can at least try, if that's what you want."

"Yes, if it is what I want." Leah warred with what she wanted and what was best for the girl. "Nelle deserves a chance to find out if she still has family."

"All right." Wesley's attention made a rapid diversion away from Leah to the road. "Do you want to come with me now or wait?"

Leah stiffened in his loose embrace. "They're here?"

After a slow nod, and his eyes focused down the road toward town, Wesley said, "Yes, it's them."

"I'll come with you."

Wesley pressed his lips to hers without a thought to who might be watching. "No matter what happens next or how hard it gets, we'll persevere together."

Wesley's arm rested at her waist when they reached the boardwalk in front of the sheriff's office and remained there after they entered the building. Peyton fed wood into the potbelly stove, bringing extra warmth to the open space. Leah tucked the paisley shawl she wore under her arms, and when doing so made her feel more vulnerable and caused an involuntary shiver, she tied the shawl ends in a loose knot in front.

"Breathe," Wesley whispered close to her ear.

Leah released the breath she hadn't realized built up in her lungs and focused on the sheriff. "Sheriff."

"Miss Tennyson. Leah." Peyton did not spare a glance for the commotion beyond the door behind him. "Forgive my bluntness, but what are you doing here?" The sheriff narrowed a look at Wesley.

"Please, do not turn your ire on Wesley. It is my decision to be here, and I intend to speak with Mr. Duggan before the day is out. If it is all the same to you, Sheriff, I prefer to do so before I leave, for I have no intention of setting eyes upon him again after today."

Wesley shrugged. "You heard her. Is there any way to bring only Duggan out here?"

Peyton slowly shook his head. "Duggan didn't make it."

Leah paled and clasped Wesley's arm for support. Wesley held her up and against him when he asked, "What happened?"

"This isn't the time, Wesley—"

"Please, I need to know." Leah straightened her legs and spine until she almost stood upright, though she still leaned on Wesley. "Is the danger to Nelle over?"

Peyton dragged a chair closer to Leah, and Wesley helped her into it. "The two men they found Duggan with are talking to Casey in their cells now. Seems they only get paid on delivery, and they'd rather make a deal to save their necks."

Leah's cheeks lost the rest of their rosy hue. Her fingers trembled as she tugged on the knotted ends of her shawl. "Delivery? You don't mean Nelle?" she whispered, her voice barely audible.

Wesley crouched in front of Leah. "This can wait."

"No, please." Leah leaned her head back to look at Peyton. "Tell us what is going on."

"Duggan tried to get off his horse when they stopped to rest the animals. He fell at an awkward angle before Carson could reach him, and his head hit a rock. They said he died instantly."

Relief washed over Leah. "Where is he?"

"They brought him back. We don't have an undertaker, so Casey took him to Emma's clinic."

"He is really gone?"

"He's gone," Peyton assured her.

Wesley brought another chair over, set it next to Leah's, and lowered himself into it. He then asked what Leah didn't want to voice. "Is Nelle still in danger?"

Peyton sat on the edge of his desk. "From what we've been able to get out of those two traveling with Duggan, a man out of Helena hired Duggan, and he in turn, hired them. They claim never to have met the Helena man."

Wesley asked, "Do you believe them?"

"About this, yes." Peyton leaned to the side to shuffle a few papers on his desk. Coming up with a crisp one, he passed it to Wesley. "Leah, I wish you'd let me spare you this."

Leah shook her head, more in control of herself now. She had only half-listened until Peyton's voice softened and hinted at a more serious turn to the conversation. "I wish I could spare myself, but I need to hear this—for Nelle."

A heavy sigh preceded Peyton's next words. "Emancipation freed the southern slaves, but unfortunately, slavery is gaining strength in the western territories." He pointed to the paper he had handed to Wesley. "That arrived last week."

"Thirteen?"

Peyton nodded. "Chinese and white women and girls found and rescued before the men could transport them to California and farther north. The youngest was twelve."

Leah stood on shaky legs, helped from her chair by Wesley. The paper crinkled in Wesley's hand when he helped Leah steady herself. "And you believe Hank Duggan was going to deliver Nelle to one of these . . . whatever or whoever?"

"This isn't the first time Duggan hired those men back there."

Moisture beaded at the edge of Leah's eyes. "Except this man who hired them doesn't know Nelle, so she should be safe. Please tell me she's safe now."

Wesley raised her chin and held her gaze. "I promise Nelle will stay safe."

Leah nodded and lowered her head to Wesley's shoulder. "I want to see her now."

"Casey wired Marshal Pinney, and he's riding out for Helena tomorrow. They'll find whoever is behind this, Leah."

Leah didn't answer. She let Wesley walk her away from the jail, yet rather than returning to the inn, he led her toward a meadow where afternoon dew from the earlier rain glistened on the tips of spring grass, dampening her skirt as they walked. "Where are we going?"

"Not far and nowhere in particular." Wesley twined her fingers with his, their palms pressing, and occasionally brushing against her hip or his thigh. "It never occurred to me that Nelle wouldn't be safe out here. My ignorance might have gotten us both killed."

"You shouldn't have to think about those things, Leah. I wish you had walked out of the sheriff's office before Peyton said anything."

"I won't remain ignorant, Wesley." She tightened her grip on his hand. "I want to protect Nelle and all the girls like her from ever facing such a danger, except it is not within my power, is it?"

Wesley stopped near a trio of aspen trees with the mountains beyond behind him and the village far enough away, so the sounds of town life faded into the air before reaching them. "To protect Nelle? You've already proven you can protect. You already have. The rest of them? Don't accept that burden, Leah. It will crush you."

A host of sparrows flew from the trees, looped through the air, and glided over the meadow. "To be so free." Leah sighed. "I sound defeated, but I am not."

Wesley brushed his fingers through the loose hair at her neck. "I know."

"What comes next?"

The gentle touch of Wesley's lips against hers silenced all doubt about what came next for either of them. As he drew her in closer, her heart raced, and the world around them seemed to fade away as they lost themselves in the sweet embrace of the kiss. All doubts and fears disappeared, replaced with a newfound sense of certainty, security, and hope.

THREE NIGHTS LATER, WITH the moon high in the night sky surrounded by a cascade of shimmering stars, Wesley stood at the bank of the brook near the inn. The air was still and the night silent, except for the occasional call of an owl in the distance and the gentle lapping of water as it flowed over and around rocks and grass.

"You should know better than to sneak up on a man at night."

Michael chuckled and completed his approach. "With another man, perhaps. With you, I'll take my chances."

"You haven't lost your skills for tracking."

"Yet you heard me."

Wesley nodded in absentmindedness, his thoughts too

disordered of late. "Only because I've been listening for everything."

"Which is why I'm here." Michael handed Wesley a folded half sheet of paper. "This arrived half an hour ago. I would have told you sooner, but it took the telegraph operator a while to find Peyton. It was addressed to him."

Wesley accepted the paper and opened it. "Telegram from the marshal." The unyielding constriction holding his chest hostage the past three days eased its grip. "They found him."

Michael nodded. "The telegram lacks details, but Casey will send another when he has more to share. Peyton thought you should be the one to tell Leah."

"I appreciate that." Wesley glanced through the trees at the inn, the place he'd begun to think of as home. During his every attempt to untangle his disorderly musings, he at no time questioned how much he wanted to remain in Crooked Creek. He said goodbye to his life in Virginia when he boarded the first train west, and never once considered returning. Except he would, if that's what Leah wanted.

"Have you told her?"

Wesley held the telegraph between two fingers and stared at Michael.

"I don't mean the good news. Have you told her about yourself?"

"Did you tell Clara everything about yourself?" Wesley countered. "No one should ever have to hear the things we did and witnessed."

"I told Clara enough so she could at least understand me, but no, I didn't tell her everything." Michael bent, picked up a fallen branch the tip of his boot nudged, and tossed it to the other side of the brook. "Clara worries about Leah. They all do, but Clara sees her growing more anxious every hour."

"She needs to know Nelle is truly safe. Casey's telegram will help."

"I used to have nightmares."

Wesley studied his old comrade and friend. "Used to?"

Michael gave him a weak smile. "Clara's love healed a lot of open wounds I carried after the war. Yours have had more time to fester. I know you spend most of your nights out on the porch than in the bed upstairs."

Wesley blew out a breath. "I have never been so certain of what I want."

"What's holding you back?"

"How can I offer her everything she deserves when their faces still haunt me? Until I learn how to let them go—"

"You won't." Michael cupped his friend's shoulder. "Who have you talked to since you returned home?"

"There was no one left who I trusted enough." Wesley returned his gaze to the inn. A flame flickered low in a lantern next to the front door. "Until now."

"I'll leave you to that."

Wesley heard rather than watched Michael leave the secluded area by the water and make his way toward the front of the inn. Only when he was once again left in solitude did Wesley realize that the worries and speculations plaguing him these past nights no longer consumed the forefront of his mind. He walked from the shadow of darkness into the lantern's dim light.

Sunlight glinted off spring leaves every time a branch swayed a little in the breeze. Wesley stirred from beneath the heavy white quilt with an eight-pointed star of red and green spreading out from the center. He could not recall how he had fallen asleep the night before, but only an overwhelming sense of hope could account for the dreamless sleep.

Wesley remembered the silence that greeted him when he finally entered the inn the night before. Prudence demanded he not go in search of Leah, though when he had stopped in the hallway in front of her door and hovered his hand ready to knock, it required a surrender to his inner angel to continue walking to his own room.

The ticking clock on the bureau across the room proved the morning had advanced later than he realized. Seven hours of sleep was a luxury unbeknownst to him since before the war. He spread an arm wide and rested it below the pillow next to him. The outline of her face filled in with soft, fair skin tinged with a faint rosy flush at her cheeks. She rested upon one open palm and locks of her hair, flecked with shades of oak and cinnamon. Her other hand lay close to his, and though his imagination had conjured a dream worthy of the word, Wesley knew it compared nothing to having her beside him in truth.

He scrubbed both hands over his unshaven face and through his hair. When he dropped his arms back to the quilt, the vision was gone and birds beyond the glass window chirped and welcomed the new day.

Wesley pushed off the quilt, sat up, and swung his legs over the side. Exhaustion kept him from moving because his mind and body had tasted of restful slumber and now ached for more of it. After several minutes, Wesley pushed off the bed, completed his morning routine, taking time to shave, and once dressed, made his way downstairs.

No sooner had he entered the dining room when Clara urged him to sit, poured fresh coffee into a mug, and warned him not to move. He chuckled before he set the edge of the mug to his lips, inhaled the nutty aroma, and sipped. She returned a minute later with a plate piled with a stack of four flapjacks, three strips of bacon, two sausages, and a side of scrambled eggs.

"No sense in arguing. Susan will take offense if I do not return to the kitchen later with an empty plate."

Wesley raised a brow but did not contradict his hostess. His stomach had plenty of room for the hearty meal. "Have Leah and Nelle already come down?"

Clara nodded and settled herself into the chair across from Wesley. "They finished their breakfast half past the hour and mentioned a walk in the meadow." When Wesley started to speak, Clara added, "Hattie and Carson are with them. They delivered a beef order this morning and accepted Leah's invitation to join them."

"Have you eaten?"

"I have, and so has everyone else." Clara stared at him, offering no quarter. "Nothing is left for you to do except eat, Mr. Davenport."

"Does your husband ever tell you no, Mrs. Donaghue?"

Clara's lips twitched. "Not when it is easier to acquiesce than argue."

Wesley grinned after another sip of coffee. "Your husband told you about the telegram?" Wesley asked before he cut a triangle of flapjacks soaked in syrup and savored the first fluffy bite on his tongue.

"He did, and I would have told Leah, but Nelle has been by her side since they came downstairs."

Wesley wondered how soon Clara would leave so he could do the same.

"It is no use." Clara pointed the tip of a narrow finger at Wesley's plate.

And so Wesley ate, and in between bites, enjoyed a few minutes of conversation with his old friend's charming wife, who carried most of the exchange while he finished the meal.

After the last piece of bacon was gone, Clara smiled as if she'd won a great conquest. She stood when Wesley did and lifted his empty plate onto a tray. "Nelle wanted to pick flowers, and the meadow with the most lilies growing this time of year is beyond Emma's medical clinic."

Wesley leaned forward and kissed Clara's cheek, drawing a smile of surprise. "Michael is a lucky man, Mrs. Donaghue."

"So will you be, Mr. Davenport." She squeezed his hand and nodded to the front of the house. "Now go, find Leah."

Leah fingered the lemony petal of a glacier lily, and her eyes veered upward to the mountain peaks covered in a thick layer of snow. Smaller patches of snow dotted the mountain slopes, a striking contrast to the pine-heavy inclines.

"When does the snow melt completely?"

Hattie smiled. "It doesn't, at least not all of it. I've never been as high up as those peaks, but Carson has lived in these mountains most of his life and traveled a fair distance. He says that some craters hold snow all year round. Some years it stays cold enough to see snow on the peaks in July. Beautiful, isn't it?"

"Spectacular. I have never seen the like, and I imagine such beauty makes the remoteness of this place worth living here." Leah's gaze returned to Nelle, who held a small bundle of lilies in her grasp and held one up for Carson, who accepted the flower and bowed. "He must be a wonderful father."

"A natural, but then he had wonderful role models in Casey, Peyton, and Michael."

Leah pictured Wesley among such men. He'd already proven his kindness and patience with Nelle and Alice. "How old is your son? Declan, if I recall."

"Yes, named for my father. He'll be a year old next month. He visits with Emma and Briley's children when we come to town." Hattie pointed to Carson and Nelle. "Now, he is likely teaching her all about that flower, and soon he'll move onto the grass, trees, and mountains. We should rescue her."

"She looks enthralled. Perhaps—" Leah turned at the sound of her name carried across the meadow.

Hattie smiled at the tall figure crossing the land and patted Leah's arm. "Instead, I think I'll join the flower lesson. Don't worry, we'll watch her."

Leah barely noticed when Hattie left her side. Without prompting, her legs carried her toward Wesley. When they met, he held out his hand, and she accepted. They walked side by side in silence, deeper into the blanket of lilies. They stopped on a gentle slope, and he invited her to sit on the spring grass.

He surprised her by holding out two folded squares of paper. "You'll want to read these for yourself. Michael gave me the one on top last night. The other he passed to me before I came out here. It had just come through over the wire."

Leah unfolded and read the first one and covered her mouth after a gasp escaped. "They caught the man?"

"Read the next one."

She quickly unfolded it and skimmed her eyes over the short telegram. "Are you certain they intended for you to let me read this?"

Wesley shrugged. "Probably not, but under the circumstances, I figured seeing the words might make it more real."

Leah brought her legs toward her chest and rested her clutched hands on her knees. "It does." She stared at the crumbled paper in her fist and immediately relaxed her fingers. "He killed himself because he couldn't have Nelle?"

Wesley uncurled her fingers from around the telegrams, removed the paper, and tucked them into his jacket pocket. "No, he killed himself because he knew what fate awaited him."

"The telegram doesn't say who *he* was."

"A businessman who believed he could buy anything and anyone. Does his name matter?" Wesley brushed a few errant strands of Leah's hair from her face. She closed her eyes and welcomed the gentleness of his touch. "Nelle's safe, Leah."

For now, she wanted to say, then realized how dispirited the words sounded. Instead, she leaned into Wesley and rested her head on his shoulder. "Yes, my Nelle is safe."

Wesley's arm wrapped around her back and made slow traces up and down her arm while the mild breeze brushed over the meadow and around them. Leah closed her eyes and breathed in the pine-scented air. "Does this moment have to end?"

"No."

Leah raised her head, though remained close to his side, and studied his face. "You mean that."

"My family owned a general store there in Washington, Virginia. Three months before Lee surrendered, a small group plundered the store and burned it down with my mother and father inside. When I returned home two weeks later, I buried them, tore down what remained of the store, and rebuilt." Wesley stared into the distance, not at any one thing from what Leah could tell. "My father suffered a limp that kept him from fighting, and though I kept my gratitude quiet, I'd never been more thankful that he didn't have to leave my mother. At least they were together, in the end."

Wesley pushed off the ground and stood, swiping grass from his pants more in frustration than out of need. "I built the store twice as big as the first one, determined to prove to the men who'd killed my parents that nothing they or anyone like them did could defeat us."

Leah ached to hold him. Instead, she let the anger inside him work its way out.

"In truth, they did defeat me, Leah. My hate for them defeated me. I worked in that store from sunup to sundown every day except Sunday, until one night at home, I laid in bed, stared at the ceiling, and couldn't remember the past two years. That's when I received Michael's letter." Wesley held his hand for Leah to take, and he helped her to her feet. "I sold the store, came out west, and then you happened."

She cupped the side of his face against her palm. "I understand anger, Wesley. When my parents died on the ship crossing from England. My sixteenth birthday passed the month before, and the excitement of traveling to America overshadowed any fear about the open sea. A storm churned for days before it stunned the ship during the night when we were all abed. My father went to help—they needed all able-bodied men on the deck. He was swept over the edge, and my mother caught a fever and passed a week later."

The soft caress of Wesley's finger beneath her eye to wipe away the moisture was the first Leah became aware of her tears. "They were the last people I truly loved until Nelle. Until you. If we cannot find Nelle's aunt, I wish to keep her with me here in Crooked Creek."

Wesley brushed both sides of her face and neck until his strong hands rested on her shoulders. "We could spend months or years waiting and learning about each other, but I already know everything important about you, everything that matters most." He brought her hands to his lips and brushed a kiss over each one. "Will you let me love you and spend every day becoming the man you deserve?"

"You already are." Leah wrapped her arms around his neck, raised onto her toes, and welcomed his kiss.

———

"Do you have everything?"

Nelle nodded and swiped a tear from her eye before it fell. "Mrs. Peyton sewed me more dresses than I can wear in a year." She stepped forward and hugged Leah in a tight embrace. "You don't have to be sad for me, Leah." Nelle stepped back and this time she wore a brilliant smile. "My aunt and her husband are real nice." She leaned in and whispered, "And fancy, too."

Leah laughed and straightened Nelle's hat. "They are indeed, and most importantly, they are good people. We made certain of it."

Wesley stood beside Leah and enjoyed the interchange, though he knew how much it cost his wife to wear a smile while fighting bruises to her heart. It took only one month after inquiries were sent throughout the territory. Elation for Nelle's good fortune and a touch of sorrow for their temporary family arrived with an unexpected telegram from Wesley's old army commander—still in Boise—who knew Nelle's aunt or rather her husband. She was now Mrs. Dunstan, wife to a wealthy timber and land developer in Oregon, and mother to two grown children.

The past two weeks they'd spent in the Dunstan's company had convinced Leah and everyone else who met them that the best part of Nelle's life was just beginning.

Leah brought Nelle close once more, held her in a fierce hug, and kissed her cheek before releasing her. "What adventures you will have, my sweet girl."

"Aunt Molly said we can come back for visits, and maybe you can come visit us sometime?" Nelle's voice held a hint of a plea with the excitement. "She said they can see the ocean from their house."

Wesley brought Leah against him to keep her steady and smiled at Nelle. "Of course we'll come visit. We already worked it out with your aunt. They're expecting us end of the summer."

"Nelle, dear. It's time to go." Molly Dunstan looked younger than her thirty-five years and wore kindness like a second coat. "Go and get in the stagecoach while I speak with Leah and Wesley."

Nelle held her arms wide for one last hug from Wesley and Leah before rushing to the coach where Mr. Dunstan waited to help her climb up. She waved energetically through the window before disappearing inside.

Molly Dunstan reached for Leah's hands, though included them both in her words. "You will be in my prayers every night. Words alone cannot express my gratitude for you and what you have done for my niece."

"It is no more than she has done for us." Leah and Molly embraced, each allowing their eyes to fill with moisture.

"We will expect you the first week of August," Molly said, before waving goodbye and joining Nelle in the coach, followed by her husband.

Wesley and Leah stood for several minutes, long after the

stage rolled out of sight, and even longer after the sound of horses' hooves and circling wheels faded into the morning.

"How is it possible to have so much joy in my heart for her and so much sadness for myself? It is selfish, I know, and yet, I miss her so much already."

Wesley kissed Leah's temple and urged her to walk away from the road. He led her toward the meadow, with grass now a foot high and wild lupine coloring the landscape. "Do you remember what I told you the day we married, when we stood before the reverend?"

"As if you spoke them only this morning."

"I vow to always love and cherish you, to be your faithful partner in life, to make you laugh and bring joy to your life, and I will love you unconditionally and with all my heart. So long as we have each other, nothing is impossible."

The words replayed in his mind even as she recounted them aloud. "I meant every word, Leah. Nothing is impossible. No matter who else we welcome into our lives, the place in our hearts we gave to Nelle will remain hers."

"No matter who else we welcome?"

Wesley studied her carefully, and when she bit her lower lip to keep from smiling, he pressed a grinning kiss to her lips. "Are you sure? This soon?"

"Emma calls it a suspicion. I call it a certainty."

Wesley lifted her in his arms and spun her in slow circles, his laughter loud enough to encourage a nearby flock of birds into flight. When he lowered her to her feet and kept her pressed to his chest, he whispered, "Thank you, Leah, for being you."

Her presence inspired him to never forget that life burned

brighter than death, and none of the horrific memories once burrowed in his heart were stronger than faith. She embodied love, kindness, and compassion, and he wanted her to know she had saved him. We have time, he thought, as they returned at a leisurely pace to Crooked Creek and embraced a new day in the rest of their lives.

ALSO BY MK MCCLINTOCK

Montana Gallaghers

Gallagher's Pride

Gallagher's Hope

Gallagher's Choice

An Angel Called Gallagher

Journey to Hawk's Peak

Wild Montana Winds

The Healer of Briarwood

Christmas in Briarwood

Crooked Creek

The Women of Crooked Creek

Christmas in Crooked Creek

British Agents

Alaina Claiborne

Blackwood Crossing

Clayton's Honor

The Ghost of Greyson Hall

McKenzie Sisters

The Case of the Copper King

And More

Hopes and Dreams in Whitcomb Springs

A Home for Christmas

ABOUT THE AUTHOR

MK McClintock is an award-winning author who writes historical romantic fiction about chivalrous men and strong women who appreciate chivalry. Her stories of romance, mystery, and adventure sweep across the American West to the Victorian British Isles with places and times between and beyond. MK enjoys a quiet life in the northern Rocky Mountains.

Visit her at **mkmcclintock.com**, where you can learn more about her books, explore reader extras, and subscribe to receive news.